A. L. Ferry

Phrenology Made Easy

A new system of mental science. Second Edition

A. L. Ferry

Phrenology Made Easy
A new system of mental science. Second Edition

ISBN/EAN: 9783337390426

Printed in Europe, USA, Canada, Australia, Japan

Cover: Foto ©Andreas Hilbeck / pixelio.de

More available books at **www.hansebooks.com**

A

NEW SYSTEM OF MENTAL SCIENCE

BY

A. L. FERRY

WASHINGTON, D. C.

(SECOND EDITION, REVISED.)

CINCINNATI:
ROBERT CLARKE & CO.
1886.

This is really a revised work from a former edition [see press notices below], which unfavorable circumstances compelled the author to complete hastily, and which he afterward found to be unsatisfactory, and consequently suppressed it. The system of mental science presented in the two editions is the same, the chief differences being slight alterations in the method of presentation, and that the substance of the first has been explained more in detail in this, and hence rendered far more comprehensive to the average reader.

PRESS NOTICES.

"A 'New System of Mental Science,' written and published by Professor A. L. Ferry, the author, who is an Emersonian student of ability, gives us a new system of Phrenology that is at once ingenious and interesting."—*Washington Sunday Gazette.*

"A little volume written by A. L. Ferry renders the study of Phrenology comparatively easy."—*The Capital (Washington).*

PREFACE.

"*Multum in parvo*," much in little, is the author's motto in the preparation of his work. I have endeavored to present in a simple and comprehensive form the underlying principles of what may justly be said to be the most accurate system of mental science which has yet been presented to the reading public or taught by teachers, taking the liberty of introducing several new features in the way of grouping and explaining the various faculties previously discovered and located in the head, and at the same time to present a conception of a harmonious development, which my observations have proven to me to be the true one, which is also apparently more in accord with Nature's universal rule of order, symmetry, and balance, than that heretofore advanced. I arrived at this conception after years of observation and study toward the one particular end, realizing that it is as impossible to teach or to arrive at any thing like accurate conclusions in regard to character from a study of the head without first having a standard of excellence or harmony, as it is to measure grain without having a standard bushel measure. I was greatly aided in my studies by two courses of instruction (in 1881 and 1884) taken in the American Institute of Phrenology in New York city; but I remained as much in the dark, in regard to this special point when I graduated as I had been when I entered, personal observation and study from life having taught me that the head presented by them as their ideal did not in a number of particulars correspond with the true proportions as discovered to accompany a harmonious character. I hope I have made the following explanations clear enough to leave the impression that there is at least a strong plausibility as to the correctness of my assumptions, and if the study of the principles hereinafter set forth be followed by careful observations with the view of testing the accuracy of my standard, I believe that it will be universally indorsed.

THE AUTHOR.

DRAWING A.

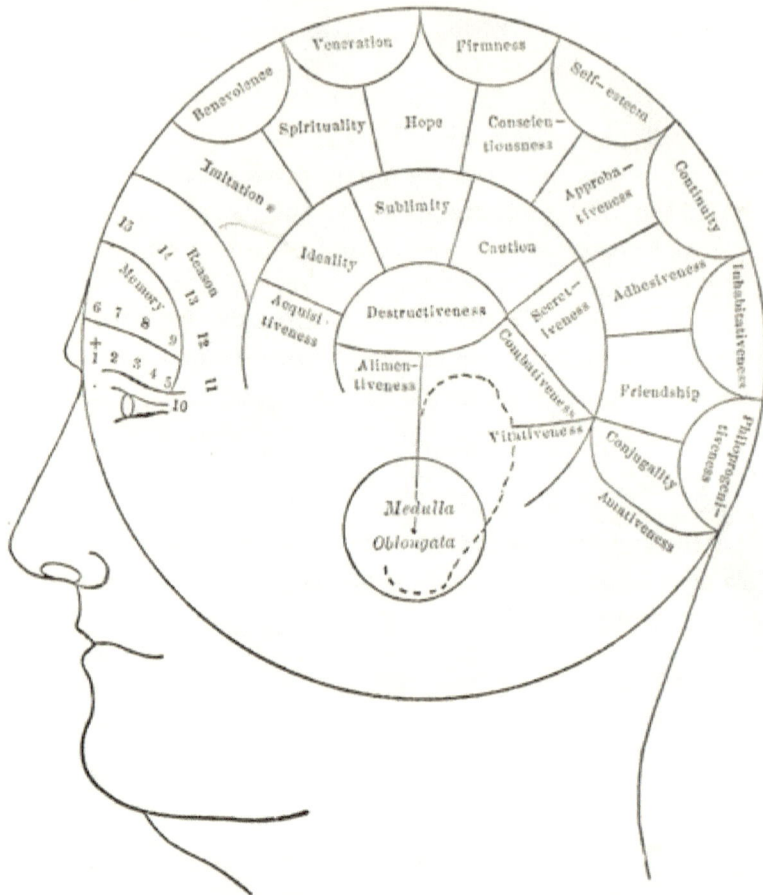

The above drawing shows the location of the faculties in a harmoniously developed head, while Drawing B, on page vi, represents the location of the different groups. (See detailed explanation of both faculties and groups on pages 19–27, inclusive.)

I do not pretend to know the size or shape of the above located faculties, but judging from Nature's universal system of balance and harmony, the function performed by each faculty being indispensable, have considered them of equal size and like form. Whether that form is square or round, or star-shaped, proving to be so many stars in the firmament of human excellencies, probably no one knows of any means of determining.

CONTENTS.

CHAPTER I.
PROGRESSION vs. MENTAL SCIENCE.

CHAPTER II.
HOW HISTORY PROVES PHRENOLOGY.

CHAPTER III.
BENEFITS OF PHRENOLOGY.

CHAPTER IV.
INTELLECTUAL FACULTIES (*Perceptives and Memory*).

CHAPTER V.
INTELLECTUAL FACULTIES (*Reasoning and Semi-intellectual Groups*).

CHAPTER VI.
THE SENTIMENTS.

CHAPTER VII.
GENERAL REMARKS.

CHAPTER VIII.
PHRENOLOGY EXPLAINED.

CHAPTER IX.
CHART—EXPLANATION.

CHAPTER X.
CHARACTER vs. HEALTH—HEALTH vs. FOOD.

DRAWING B.

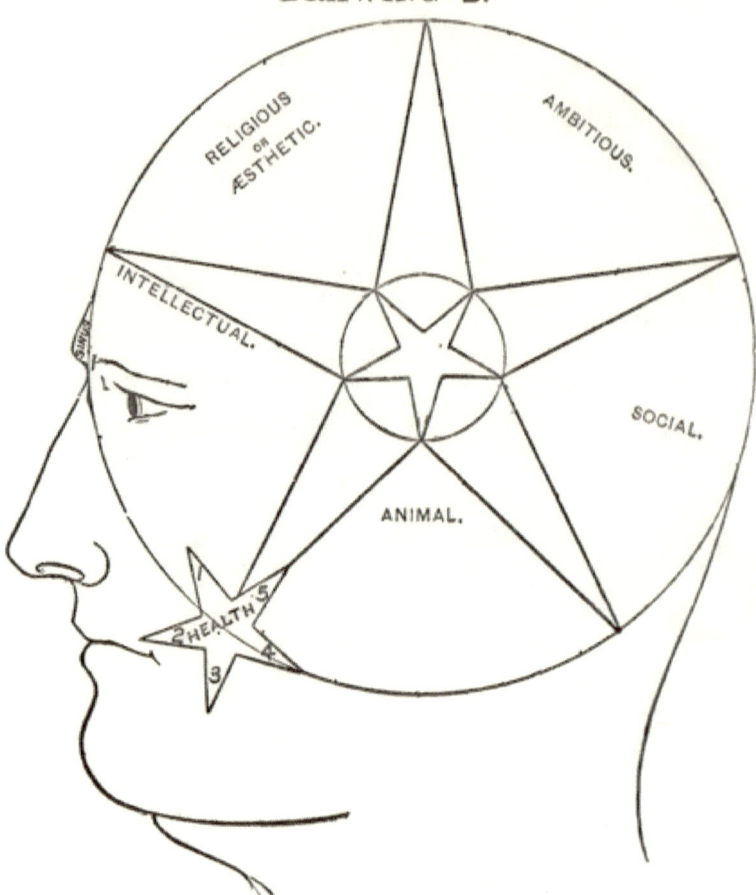

The above cut shows the different natures of man, which are composed of so many groups of faculties. In the explanation of these natures, and the faculties which constitute or serve them, I employ another group, named the "Semi-Intellectual" faculties; but as they do not represent a special nature, merely joining or lying between the "Animal" and the four other groups, I omitted it in the above drawing.

The star in the face represents the five physiognomical signs by which to determine health. A careful Phrenologist will pay as much attention to health as to shape of head, for it is a very essential element in character and abilities. For full explanation of these health signs see chapter IX.

CHAPTER I.

PROGRESSION vs. MENTAL SCIENCE.

"Undeveloped intellect, be it that of an individual or that of a race, form conclusions which require to be revised and revised before they reach a tolerable correspondence with realities."—*Herbert Spencer.*

It is now over a century since it was discovered by Dr. Gall* that certain cranial peculiarities were accompanied by certain physical manifestations, which led him to enter deeply into a study of human nature, aided by the new method of searching for special actions corresponding with cranial development, and cranial development corresponding with special actions, thus proving beyond a doubt (what was then a much mooted question) that the brain, located in the skull, was the seat of the mind, and also that the mind had special organs to direct and control certain actions, as independently as the different members of the body performed special or separate duties.

Dr. Gall named and located a number of the mental faculties, describing their corresponding influence in the character, which forms the foundation or basis of the present well-known system of Phrenology.

Since Dr. Gall's time many additional discoveries have been made by his followers, as well as numerous attempts toward the systematic organization of the faculties into groups, and the formation of many theories in regard to the influence upon and the relation to each other of the various organs of the mind.

That Phrenologists have succeeded in obtaining many accurate ideas, proved by the truly remarkable delineations of

---

* Dr. Gall was born in Germany in 1758. His first studies were for the priesthood, which studies he afterward discontinued, entered a medical college, and was graduated a regular physician (and in Germany they *educate* their physicians). He afterward served as physician in ordinary to the Emperor. Dr. Gall named and located twenty-six faculties.

the characters of entire strangers by some of the most expert practitioners, has been too often demonstrated to need comment, while the fact that there are many defects in the present theories and systems is noticeable from the generally mixed up conception in the minds of the multitude of "bumpology"* as Phrenology, and also in the reason that so important a factor as a reliable method of becoming acquainted with character, as this really is, would have been in more general use had its true principles been presented in a simple, accurate, and comprehensive manner.

It would be foolish to claim that mind or human nature can not be studied otherwise than by the aid of Phrenology, for many valuable metaphysical works have been produced by writers who have ably and logically reasoned from effect to cause—*i. e.*, from human actions to the probable motives that must have caused them—and the writers who are considered the deepest thinkers of the ages (among others, Plato, Swedenborg, and later, Emerson, the "Sage of Concord") have each produced elaborate treatises on different branches of this subject; but the system of mental science that can explain, as well as give a means of determining the relative size, and hence influence, in individuals, of the different desires and faculties which cause all the manifestations about which these great minds have been puzzled, must necessarily underlie all of their works, and that is what can be reasonably claimed for the system herein presented; and it may also be asserted that when this system has been carefully studied, and its principles comprehended, students will find the works of those writers far more easy to understand than they would be without this aid.

A careful study of the different writings of noted mental and moral philosophers can not fail to further explain the principles or general truths hereinafter set forth, for they will be found to take up and explain various branches of this all-underlying subject; for the study of mind necessarily entails the study of all the manifestations of mind, as are found in every thing that bears the stamp of man's restless genius.

* See "BUMPS" in Chapter VIII.

CHAPTER II.

HOW HISTORY PROVES PHRENOLOGY.

"The world exists for the education of each man. There is no age or state of society or mode of action in history to which there is not something corresponding in his life. . . . He should see that he can live all history in his own person. . . . All history becomes subjective; in other words there is properly no history, only biography."—*Emerson.*

TURNING to history, we may almost see the growth of man's several natures, as well as faculties, in the progress of time. Especially is it seen in the earliest and most complete, and also what is considered the most accurate, of all ancient histories, the Bible, which seems to record the manifestations of man's loftiest, as well as his lowest or animal sentiments—the former in individuals, the latter in races.

The records of man in the antediluvian period, with rare exceptions of individual excellence, might be supposed to describe the actions of the highest race of animals designated as belonging to the brute creation, the animal wants, or the wants of the faculties hereinafter attributed to the animal nature, being gratified independent of all other considerations.

Then came the growth of the social faculties, man seeking a single mate or partner (Conjugality), and gradually condemning promiscuous sexual relations. With that partnership came the special love of and care and attention to offspring (Philoprogenitiveness)—which seemed formerly merely to be a temporary duty of the female, but now fulfilled and continued through life by both sexes. It is of this era in which the record mentions how they gloried in, and considered themselves blessed by, having "many sons and daughters."

This love probably led to the banding together of the individuals into tribes and races for protection, and resulted in the development of a new tie of affection (Friendship), also to the selection of a permanent residence or home (Inhabitativeness), to which they afterward became as warmly attached as to either wife, children, or friends, calling into action that adhesive or lasting friendship (Adhesiveness), which caused them to sacrifice every thing held dear, if necessary, for friends.

This constant love of friends and home seems to be something higher than mere animal love, and we find that such personal strifes as that of "Jacob and Esau" (unless as the representatives of divisions of people), receive less attention, and instead, the strifes of tribes and races, and instances cited of lofty patriotism so inspiring individuals that at times life, wife, children, friends, all seem forgotten in the overmastering devotion to "my country," and the "land of my birth."

Seemingly as aids in the protection of and provision for these new wants are developed "Secretiveness" (or the power to use strategy or practice slyness as an agent in self-preservation, in connection with "Destructiveness" and "Combativeness," the two faculties, classed among the "Animal" group, which give the destroying or executing, and the aggressive tendencies, thus adding *discretion* to *valor*), and "Acquisitiveness," the ability to secure and hoard some thing which may prove a reserve fund in case of possible contingencies—such as war, famine, or climatic severities.

The growth or increase in the development of the intellect is going on all this time, as necessarily excited into continuous activity by these new desires.

The senses, which give the perception of things through their numerous qualities, commence to search for more information to be employed by the utilizing faculties, "Calculation" being necessary to determine the number of things necessary to supply the general wants, and to estimate when that number is secured, while "Constructiveness" conceives of different forms of arrangement in which they will best answer the required ends, the hand becoming skillful in modeling according to such conceptions.

As memory of events or occurrences (Eventuality), of localities or places (Locality), of lapses of time connected with occurrences and with sound (Time and Tune), and the association of sounds with objects (Language), so as to be better able to describe that which is desired, and have increased powers of communication and expression, were all employed, we can realize the birth, growth, and extension of language, and the formation of history.

The possession of a development, however slight, of each of the "Animal," "Social," and "Intellectual" faculties so far mentioned, by some of the higher grades of the brute creation has been discovered, although there are but few instances in which they were all possessed and exercised together by a single specie; but when the above has been said, it may also be affirmed that there has been no further manifestations by them which can not be explained as the separate or combined action of those faculties, unless it is a slight tinge of "Causality" and "Comparison" in dogs, which are considerably in and seem to enjoy the society of man—causality making them appreciate man's superiority, and comparison detecting some resemblances between individuals, thus being enabled to receive impressions as to character—but it is extremely doubtful. The assertion has probably never been made that any one of the lower animals has ever shown signs that it was conscious of the incongruities which to us seem ridiculous, and so often broaden man's face with a smile or convulse him with laughter.

"Wit" gives the perception of incongruities, "Causality," the power for deep and logical deductions from effect to cause, and "Comparison," the ability for comparative or analogous reasoning, finding in one thing the key by which to explain another. These seem to be attributes of man's higher natures—namely, his "Ambitious" and "Religious or Æsthetic" sentiments—rather than of those hereinbefore described.

If we admit that there is an incongruity, it follows that man must needs possess a sense of something signifying harmony, for if there was no appreciation of the existence of harmony there could be no power to detect incongruity, these terms having comparative meanings. A faculty, "Ideality," appears to appreciate certain approaches to harmony, without the conception of a universal harmony which belongs to "Sublimity," and for the exercise or gratification of which latter faculty man seems to turn away from his own works to seek in the perfumes, the sunshine, and the zephyrs, amidst the ever-changing shades of light and shadow and varying colors of the dancing green leaves and swaying grass-blades and flowers, while being serenaded by Nature's grand orchestra, the music resulting from the melodious concord of bird and insect voices, which appear to swell the chorus in a grander requiem than he can comprehend in its entirety, and must at present be content merely to enjoy. Is it surprising that with these new conceptions should come a feeling of awe or fear, such as is probably the function of "Caution"?

I may seem to have digressed from my subject; but it was of the utmost importance to notice the development of these faculties, for with such development came the birth of art and poetry.

The first works of art were mainly the formation of images, either entirely resembling the lower animals, or possessing partly human and partly animal characteristics; but it was not until the breath of inspiration was caught from the higher conception of the "Religious or Æsthetic" faculties that we have an account of a really idealistic production, which has been handed down to us in the detailed description of the construction of the "Ark of the Covenant" under the supervision of the world's first sage—MOSES—which not only shows artistic workmanship, but through its symbols flows into poetry. Thus it is seen that art, though first attempted by idol-worshipers, needed the higher conception of an invisible and all-ruling God to raise it to a superior degree of beauty and excellence.

Whether it was through the perception of his own present incongruity with the highest in Nature (Wit), the spirit of inquiry as to whether things were as they should be and a wondering what every thing means and logical deductions for causes (Causality), and a resulting search through all forms and conditions for resemblances and explanations (Comparison), as skeptics might believe to be the cause of the birth and growth of these higher natures; or that the natural germination of the inherent and divinely-planted germs of a great desire to be something higher, something grander, and an inexplicable belief in a something higher and grander—even an immortality of happiness—caused to be developed the above mentioned specially human or superior intellectual powers, to search for means of reaching or knowing more of such grandeur, as others are inclined to believe—it matters but little, for it arrives at the same end; but past as well as present history leaves not the slightest doubt but that there have appeared individuals who believed in grand laws of right and justice (Conscientiousness), believed in their continued influence through time and eternity (Firmness), believed that they were for themselves and their kindred specially (Self-esteem), and that all other people and nations should appreciate the fact of their individual greatness, and be submissive and pay their respects to or worship them accordingly (Approbativeness), and showed a steady adherence to this belief, and possessed a power of continued application to means for compelling such submission (Continuity)—for they stand out conspicuously, as well as that individuals with all these characteristics could also appreciate others' excellencies (Imitation ∗), had conceptions which seemed to stretch into infinitude (Spirituality), feeling pity for and exercising charity toward those less favored (Benevolence), with a boundless hope or feeling of certainty that present life serves but as an avenue or gateway to blessings and beauties untold (Hope), and believing that there is a great God, the designer of the universe, who is waiting with extended arms to welcome His struggling children when they have faithfully done their best toward preparing this earth and its inhabitants to serve a still inscrutable purpose (Veneration).

Men possessed of large developments of one or two of these natures, with an intellectual ability and the necessary vitality to give them power, have committed deeds of oppression or achieved victories which have attracted the attention and dazzled the minds of the whole civilized race, making them wonder at or stand in awe of their prowess; but the few who have had the "Social," "Ambitious," and the "Religious or

Æsthetic" sentiments strongly developed and evenly balanced, with enough of the animal nature to sustain mighty efforts, although standing so entirely alone that they have had few or no followers to defend them when the most ignorant classes were stirred up through fear and jealousy to destroy them, have afterward been remembered and worshiped as Gods.

Although each progressive epoch of history is marked by the development and influence of these different faculties in the human family as races, yet in our present advanced state of civilization separate individuals can be found who, as far as feeling or sentiment is concerned, are representative of the ruling characteristics of the different grades of history which have been noticed; but the majority of such individuals are capable of intellectually approving higher laws of justice and humanity than their inner nature, as at present developed, would have prompted them to adopt, and with the fear of the punishment entailed by our laws for the violation of certain principles, influencing them, are found to be not only law-abiding but industrious and hard-working, and hence valuable citizens. Being subjected for a few generations to the influences of education, and intermarrying with higher or oppositely developed persons, seems sufficient to raise such natures to the average development represented in this age.

Whether any individual yet born has combined in himself an even and powerful development of all of these natures, including the "Animal" and "Intellectual," is extremely doubtful. Probably the world is yet at too infantile a stage of growth, and its inhabitants have not yet secured the knowledge which will probably be necessary to produce as well as nourish this child of the ages, whose coming has already been prophesied.

CHAPTER III.

BENEFITS OF PHRENOLOGY.

"I declare myself a hundred times more indebted to Phrenology than to all the metaphysical works I ever read. . . . I look upon Phrenology as the guide to philosophy and the handmaid of Christianity. . . . Whoever disseminates true Phrenology is a true benefactor."—*Horace Mann.*

WHEREIN the greatest benefits are derived from Phrenology would be hard to determine. They are undeniably reformatory, inasmuch as the better knowledge we have of the inner motives that prompt human actions, the less we are inclined to condemn, and the more to pity, aid, and encourage the unfortunate.

"Know thyself!" has long been used as a maxim proverbial of the most important of all knowledge; but is it more important than to have a knowledge of your relation to your fellow-man, which can only be obtained when you understand your fellow-man by appreciating the motives which prompt his actions, which actions so often cause unnecessary misunderstandings? It is not even enough that one man can understand others, but that they can in turn understand him, before a community can work together with tolerable harmony. There is no other single study which will aid in the securing of such knowledge as will Phrenology. If we could imagine a relevant flash of light traversing the earth and discovering to each person all the weaknesses of his character, would it not produce fearfully depressing results? But the old world would rally and go on as before; and if another flash would come and reveal a certain mode of bettering existing conditions, would they not afterward dance to a livelier strain? These flashes are bound to and have come in the way of knowledge, and we turn to thank God who sends them.

"What good is a delineation and chart; do you think you know me better than I know myself?" is an oft-repeated question. In regard to the latter part of the inquiry we may emphatically assert that in nine cases out of ten we do. " Well, if you do, that will not help matters," may be replied. Your knowing yourself will help matters *independent* of its aid to self-improvement. Knowing that the leg of a chair is broken will not mend it, but it will be apt to aid you in saving yourself from many serious bruises or mishaps that might otherwise occur. The same is true when you have a chart of your character. The chart, of itself, will not improve it, but it will warn you against bearing too heavily on weak points, and especially aid you to make intellectual allowances in the formation of your judgment of persons, instead of gauging other people's desires by your own desires (as we are bound to do until science teaches us better), or condemning them as " cranky " because they see differently through their mental windows than you do through yours, while your windows may be so small and narrow as to give you but a very limited view.

As a means of self-improvement a chart and examination will direct you what class of studies will be most important toward producing a harmonious development of the intellect, and what steps to take to cultivate the sentiments, advising you how to make the most of your time if it is limited and you have general culture for your object.

A person may tread under foot untold wealth which a slight hint would enable him to discover. It is most easy to find that which is positively known to be lost.

It will prove valuable as a guide to choice of pursuit, for while a person with a harmoniously developed intellect and the necessary health and strength can be successful in almost any branch of business, trade, or profession, yet there are many necessary duties or details of some pursuits against which the inner natures or sentiments will constantly rebel, thus causing more or less unhappiness, which will not hold true in all pursuits, some of which will not only prove profitable, but will afford actual pleasure in their performance.

Those who have certain dispositions and lack a harmoniously developed intellect can have explained to them why they would not be satisfied or contented in certain employments, as well as that it would not be judicious for them to follow certain callings in the hope of meeting speedy financial success (although an application to such branches might be the very thing to aid them in self improvement), for the reason that every-where competition is liable to be too fierce and wages too low for those to gain support who have not the advantages of immediate adaptability.

Without hints or aids you may make mistakes which will be hard to remedy, for every business, trade, or profession has too many peculiarities and technicalities, of no value whatever except in connection with it, to be learned in a hurry. and your first occupation is likely to be your permanent one,

Undoubtedly the best method (if you are not independent) is to apply yourself to that which is likely to afford you the speediest pecuniary returns, and as soon as possible seek means to cultivate the faculties which will tend to produce a harmonious character, for whether you use intervening time between present hours of employment for such end, or devote your entire attention to its accomplishment after you have earned the leisure, no other labors will be so richly remunerated by blessings which may possibly be attained but which money can not buy.

Those who have already a trade or profession, and desire to gradually work out of it into something more remunerative or satisfactory, may possibly receive valuable advise or suggestions.

Of untold value is Phrenology as an aid in the treatment and culture of children. Different dispositions require different treatment, and that which is necessary to urge one child forward will impel another to constant rebellion, keeping active the worst faculties (or those which should be soothed or quieted instead of being irritated), and ultimately causing them to leave their homes, and probably be allured into any kind of excesses which will appear to offer momentary enjoyment. While some children should be urged onward in their studies, others should be taken from school and given duties which will gradually draw their mind from certain tendencies toward another or more practical acquirement, which will often save many from an early death, and give to many others increased powers, not only for work but for enjoyment, which would not otherwise have fallen to their lot.

Probably the greatest of all benefits to be derived from a knowledge of your own peculiarities of character, and a means of accurately determining the peculiarities of others' characters, is the aid it renders in the selection of a " partner for life." It is no use talking otherwise than that there is no step a person can take where a mistake is liable to be followed by so many evil consequences as the one that is so often made in marriage. That being the case, no information that tends to throw a light on this difficult problem will fail to be of infinite value, not only to the members of the present generation who shall give it proper thought, but those of the coming generations who may receive the benefits resulting from such thought by being well-born.

At first thought, with some, it may seem a queer and unnatural idea to marry persons for the shape of their heads; but second thought will show that the shape of the head is merely studied as an index to character, and who will have the levity to ridicule the idea of loving and marrying a person for the noble traits of character?

It is sure soon to become as common and seem as natural a practice to notice and even measure your sweetheart's head* as it is now to notice the beauty, erect carriage, handsome form, sweet temper, ability as a seamstress, cook, or housekeeper, of the female, and the steady habits and business capabilities of the male, as well as the prospects of either party in the " matter-of-money " (often pronounced " matrimony "), with many or all of which attributes it is now the custom to adorn a beau-ideal, and then seek some favored individual to resemble it.

Many other points—such as to notice whether the one from whom you seek information can be relied on for accuracy, or as to what are the best characteristics to seek, to offset yours, in selecting a business partner—are of considerable importance.

---

* There are other very important considerations beside shape of head—constitution, health, etc.—for remarks on which, see Chapters IX and X.

CHAPTER IV.

INTELLECTUAL FACULTIES.

PERCEPTIVES AND MEMORY.

"We have five senses : seeing, hearing, feeling, tasting, and smelling. When we see, feel, taste, or smell things or hear sounds, we are said to perceive them. I drop a book upon the floor. A force, called gravitation, draws it toward the center of the earth. We can not perceive this force, but we are conscious of it—that is, we know such force must exist. We are conscious of many other things that we can not perceive, as love. hatred, joy, sorrow."—*Harvey's Elementary Grammar.*

THE above are really the first principles of mental science, and as these are almost universally known, I can think of no better plan than to build this structure of mental philosophy from the above simple and acknowledged foundation.

The perception through the senses is the first manifestation of mind, and in the lowest forms of being not all of these are necessary agents for the sustenance of life—many of such lower forms being enabled to provide for their wants through the mere sense of feeling, and scientists have discovered that even plants are known to possess this sense of feeling and employ it in securing nourishment.

But my work lies not with the senses, but with the faculties which employ the impressions received through the senses for the gratification of the many wants of man, and to explain the nature of the wants or desires, which "we are conscious of" but "can not perceive."

Physiologists have determined that each of the different parts of the tongue possesses the power of detecting only a single peculiarity of taste—sweetness, sourness. bitterness,. etc.—locating these parts, thus showing the allotment of separate duties to separate parts or organs.

The duty of a Phrenologist is merely to show that the sense which is far more essential to the needs and enjoyments of man than to any of the lower animals—namely, sight—not only possesses different organs for the detection of the different qualities of a thing perceived by such sense, but that these organs are located in the skull, immediately above the eye, and their sizes can be determined by the shape or curve of the skull at this locality,* and the general length of the brain fiber from the brain-center forward to this region, the method for determining such length of fiber being carefully explained in detail on pages 44 and 45, to which the reader is referred.

[While reading the descriptions contained in the three following chapters, Drawing A, on page iv, should be frequently referred to, to find the location of the different faculties, and Drawing B, on page vi, to see the relative positions occupied by the several groups of faculties herein explained as constituting or serving the different natures.]

The qualities of an object detected by the organs so located are Form (1), Size (2), Weight (3), Color (4), and Order (5).

A full development of "Form" gives the perception as well as memory of the forms of different objects—round, square, oval, etc. It causes breadth between the eyes.†

A full development of the organ of "Size" gives perception and memory of the sizes of different objects—large, small, etc.

The faculty called "Weight" distinguishes and remembers the relation of objects to the perpendicular, and its activity is necessary to enable us to maintain our balance; it has been discovered to be remarkably developed in tight-rope walkers.

The name "Weight" is liable to deceive by leaving the impression that through it we are enabled to judge of the weight

---

* This point has been greatly disputed by physiologists who claim that the existence of a bony ridge and a cavity between the two plates of the skull at this point prevents such discernment; but this ridge and cavity present no obstacle, as they are natural formations of the skull, found in all adult heads, and the action of the brain does not extend a single plate of the skull but both plates alike, the skull retaining its natural formation. The above fact has been conclusively demonstrated by expert Phrenologists through the accuracy of their examinations in describing the relative power of the above-named organs in different individuals.

† The cause of this faculty's producing breadth is supposed to be from a peculiar formation of the inside of the skull between the eye arches.

of an object with the eye, which ability is probably largely indebted to "Size" and "Calculation," after once the memory of a certain weight associated with or as belonging to a certain size or bulk of distinct materials has been cultivated.

"Color" gives the perception and memory of the different shades or colors of an object or objects. That many show a weakness or lack of ability in this direction has been prominently brought to notice lately by accounts of railroad accidents, caused by employes being so deficient in this particular that they could not remember, and some could not even detect, the difference in the color of the signal-lights — colorblindness.

"Order" perceives and remembers a certain order or existing relation. The function of " Form," Size," Weight," and "Color," as well as that of the senses of feeling, tasting, smelling, and hearing, seems to be to merely deal with the separate qualities of things with which their names show them to be associated, without a sense of the relation of these qualities to a thing or as constituting a thing, which detection of the relation of such qualities as a thing, and probably of a certain relation existing between things themselves, is undoubtedly the function of " Order."

Although the above-described faculties are classed under the head of " Memory" in the drawing, the description shows that they partake as well of the nature of the perceptives, and are often alluded to as such.

" Individuality " (+) gives the memory of individual things, of which all qualities are attributes and constituents. When this faculty is fully developed it causes a prominence at or slightly above the point marked " 1 " in the drawing. This has been and probably may be spoken of as one of the perceptives, but it seems to partake solely of the nature of memory.

While this faculty may be spoken of as the memory of associated qualities, there has been a set of faculties discovered which deal exclusively with associated ideas, or qualities and ideas combined, the analysis of which is a very difficult matter.

The faculties for the memory of associated ideas are named Eventuality (6), Locality (7), Time (8), Tune (9), and Language (10).

"Eventuality" has been explained as the memory of events or history. A little thought will show that such memory of events must be made up from a number of associated impressions, first separately received through the senses, for such impressions are the result of an event, and when impressions or events are carefully described and commented on they become what is known as history.

"Locality" is the memory of places or localities, which can only be remembered by their surroundings—the trees, houses, fences, etc., by their color, shape, height, positions, etc. This faculty has been found remarkably developed in travelers.

"Time" has been described as being a sort of inner consciousness of lapses of time or duration, which is probably gauged by the regular heart-beat, the human time-keeper, but must be associated with forms or figures, as in dates; or words, as in days and months; or with sounds, as in music, before it gives the ability to remember the same in such connections.

"Tune" seems to be a faculty depending entirely on the sense of hearing. It gives the appreciation and memory of sound in various associations, one of which (with time) is music. This faculty does not necessarily give the ability to render vocal or instrumental music or remember tunes, those being the outcome of particular associations. The voice may be harsh, or the person with a good appreciation of sound and even tune may lack the necessary power of application, or be unable to remember or execute the necessary manipulations to produce instrumental music. While a fair development of this faculty is necessary for the musician, it has been found well developed in persons who do not show musical ability, but can remember and appreciate sounds.

"Language" is dependent upon the memory of forms of letters, their association into words of various lengths, and the association of words into sentences, as well as the peculiar sound made in pronouncing, and the length of time taken in utterance.

From this analysis it may be seen that this memory is closely allied to "Tune" and "Time," and greatly aided by " Form," "Size," and "Order," and although it is apparently located behind the eye (10) in drawing A, it is not supposed to lie below the perceptives, but that a peculiar formation of the brain above this region slightly presses the back part of the arch above the eye downward and outward, thus producing the full appearance of the eye which Dr. Gall invariably detected in his fellow-students who were distinguished for such memory. This peculiarity first excited his curiosity in regard to the relation of the mind to the shape of the head.

As the material collected and remembered by all of these organs is used as the basis from which deductions are made by the reasoning faculties, they, in turn, probably remember the different forms of such deductions. As the sentiments are gratified through the separate and combined action of the entire group of intellectual faculties, there is reason to believe that each of them performs a certain function of memory. The activity of a single faculty may indirectly have an exciting or awakening influence on the others.

CHAPTER V.

INTELLECTUAL FACULTIES.

REASONING AND SEMI-INTELLECTUAL GROUPS.

"We have no other faculties of perceiving or knowing any thing, divine or human, but by our five senses and our reason.—Peter Browne."—*Webster's Dictionary.*

The faculties employed in reasoning or deducing are Calculation (11), Constructiveness (12), Wit (13), Causality (14), and Comparison (15).

"Calculation" is a very important factor in directing human actions. It is rightly classed as one of the reasoning faculties, for it takes reason to determine that this balances that; that a certain amount of energy is required for the taking of a single step; that one thing can be put with another and result in something entirely different from either of the two composing factors; or, in other words, that two and two make four, and that four sticks attached to a board make a bench. This is one of the faculties ("Acquisitiveness," another), the true function of which seems to be almost forgotten on account of being continually associated with certain representative forms, objects, etc. (such as figures with "Calculation" and money with "Acquisitiveness"), but of which they are entirely independent.

So misleading are these associations that George Combe, an enthusiastic advocate of Phrenology, and author of his popular "Constitution of Man," seems to have erred in this particular direction. He deplored his supposed entire deficiency of this faculty because he could not learn and remember the multiplication table. This ability lies entirely with the memory, and has little or nothing to do with the act of calculating, that being performed in the application of such table in solving problems or working examples. That "Calculation" may not have been one of his strongest faculties is admissible That he had and exercised a certain development of that faculty is evident from the manner in which he so carefully weighed and balanced the points presented in the above-mentioned valuable and well-known work. A man can not take a step without calculation, and he may be a careful calculator, and even mathematician, without ever having employed a figure in his life, dealing entirely with facts, Figures are merely used to stand for or designate things or facts.

"Constructiveness" seems to partake much of the nature of "Calculation," except that it deals exclusively with complex forms and arrangements. This has been much associated with mechanism and building. While it is absolutely necessary in the use of mechanism and for the purposes of building and constructing houses, etc., it should not be forgotten that these are only conceived ideas embodied in iron and wood by the skillful mechanic. The conception is independent of all forms, and may be expressed in wood, colors, words, etc.

The special function of " Wit" seems to be to detect incongruities (as noticed on page 11). There must be a certain sense of harmony before there can be a sense of an incongruity, which implies a reasoning from one condition to another. " Wit " is found largely developed in wits or jokers, and in eminent artists as well. Jokers, as a rule, do not laugh more or as much as others, but seem to see and describe the ridiculous side of things to make others laugh.

Volumes might be and probably are written on the subject of " Why We Laugh ? "—and yet, who knows ? We laugh at others mistakes, discovering that some one else or something is out of harmony, we, of course, being in harmony (for the time being, at least), which seems to make us feel "good" or "better," and we have to give vent to our ecstacy in laughter, as Addison reasoned in his *Spectator;* but that does not fill the entire bill by any means· There seems to be some thing in the mere meeting of acquaintances or loved ones provocative of mirth, and such meeting can surely not always be a mistake. A harmonious development of all our natures, good digestion, general health and strength, and the proper exercise of all of our various faculties seem to be essential to our enjoyment and happiness, and hence make us feel like laughing. This manifestation can not well be attributed to a single faculty of "Mirthfulness," as it has been.

The special function of reasoning performed by "Causality," seems to be the abstract, or from effect to cause and from cause to effect, in an endeavor to satisfy the insatiable desire in man to know what every thing neans: implying an innate belief that every thing has a hidden meaning.

"Comparison" has already been spoken of in Chapter II in connection with analogous reasoning and the study of human nature. It will be observed by those acquainted with the old system that I have omitted to mark in my drawing a supposed faculty called "Human Nature." The definition given of this faculty is that through it we possessed an intuitive and inexplicable power of detecting or understanding human nature- It may be admitted that we have a special faculty for the ap. preciation of the special manifestations designated as human nature, as explained in the following chapter; but as there are no means of receiving impressions or of forming judgments except through our senses and reason, the above supposed inexplicable impressions can be explained as resulting from the combined activity of the memory and comparative reason. It is an acknowledged fact that like thoughts produce like actions, like habits producing like people. This is observed in races as well as individuals. Certain resemblances between a stranger and some one formerly known may cause an impression as to character—often accurate, sometimes erroneous.

The Semi-Intellectual group embraces Acquisitiveness, Secretiveness, Caution, Ideality, and Sublimity.

"Acquisitiveness" seems to give the ability to acquire and hold. It is apparently the working together of the animal nature and the intellect—intellect being necessary to get, and animal selfishness being necessary to retain.

"Secretiveness" gives the inclination toward and power to employ policy or secrecy, so often necessary for the preservation of self and those dependent on you. This faculty joins the animal nature with the social.

" Caution " gives prudence or fear, and it joins or is located between the animal and ambitious natures, just where it would seem that a careful admonitor is necessary.

" Ideality " gives the love of art, which seemingly is the product of a conception of certain harmonies. It joins the animal and the moral or æsthetic nature, probably the avenue through which man climbs away from animality into a new world of higher conceptions.

" Sublimity " has been explained as giving a love for Nature. But what is it we see and love in Nature if it is not a general and universal harmony? It is not one thing or impression she regales us with, but many, all forming parts of a " perfect whole." If we do not call it harmony how can we explain the feeling of enjoyment that is caused by the swaying trees, with their leaves dancing and their branches in swinging arches, the sparkling and glistening of the water, the babbling of the brook, with the delicious perfumes, and sensitive delight from the cooling and refreshing breezes, which fan the glow of health into our cheeks.

This faculty joins the animal to the ambitious and the religious or æsthetic faculties, and is joined by "Caution" to the social and by "Ideality" to the intellectual groups.

CHAPTER VI.

THE SENTIMENTS.

" Here is an attribute which, to say the least, has had an enormous influence, . . . and is at present the life of numerous institutions, the stimulus of perpetual controversies, and the prompter of countless daily actions. Any theory of things which takes no account of these attributes, must, then, be extremely defective."—*Herbert Spencer on the Religious Sentiments.*

As much as is claimed for the religious sentiments in the above purely scientific view can be said of the ambitious, social, and animal sentiments or natures. History speaks too plainly in regard to each of their influences to leave any doubt as to their being distinct attributes of human nature.

It may be left to the naturalists to determine the truth or falsity of the broad assertion that all forms of beings represent different phases of "arrested and progressive development," or that man has advanced in ages from and through lower animal forms up to his present excellence and superiority. But it is of the *utmost* importance in the study of man to realize that he has an animal nature, not differing perceptibly from that of the lower animals, and also to appreciate the truth of the statement that to become a " great man you must first be a good animal." " There is a law of self-preservation, written by God Himself on the heart." It needs the animal nature to fulfill it; but this, in turn, must be balanced by the other natures, and all of them directed by the intellect.

The animal nature has five agents or faculties, each having a particular function to perform in the preservation of life. These faculties are Vitativeness, Alimentiveness, Destructiveness, Combativeness, and Amativeness.

"Vitativeness" gives the love of life, without which there could be no existence.

"Alimentiveness" gives the love of food and drink, which is necessary for the sustenance of life.

"Destructiveness" gives the power to destroy or execute. Man could not destroy an insect or chop down a tree of the forest without this faculty. This faculty was first called "murder," because it was found largely developed in murderers, but subsequent investigation has shown that it is not generally larger in murderers than it is in our great men. The difference in the manifestations must result from a deficiency of the higher faculties in the former. Whether this faculty commits murder or organizes and runs sunday-schools or revival meetings depends entirely upon how it is balanced by the other faculties and directed by the intellect. It is more appropriately spoken of as "Executiveness."

"Combativeness" gives the aggressive or driving tendency, but needs to be balanced by "Destructiveness" to give great executive ability. Without such balancing it almost invariably causes a great waste of force.

"Amativeness" gives the desire for and love of physical exercise. This is a different explanation of the function of this faculty than that generally given. There are many reasons to believe that the former explanation is altogether too narrow and limited.

The faculties governing man's social nature are Conjugality, Philoprogenitiveness, Friendship, Adhesiveness, and Inhabitativeness.

"Conjugality" is essentially the marriage tie, giving the love for a single mate or partner of the opposite sex.

"Philoprogenitiveness" gives the love for children and pets.

"Friendship" gives the love of friends or society.

"Adhesiveness" gives the lasting friendship. It differs from "Friendship" in that, while the latter may be satisfied with temporary friends as met in society, this gives an adhering or constant affection that can not be easily broken.

"Inhabitativeness" gives the desire for and love of a home.

As the composing faculties or agents for man's ambitious nature have been classed Continuity, Approbativeness, Self-esteem, Conscientiousness, and Firmness.

"Continuity" gives ability for the steady and unremitting application which is necessary to achieve ambitious ends.

"Approbativeness" gives the desire for the respect and admiration of others. It differs from the social faculties in that they desire companionship, while this merely craves respect.

"Self-esteem" gives the belief in self, and a desire to be "somebody."

"Conscientiousness" gives a belief in a right and a wrong, i. e., in existing laws, the obedience to which is right, the violation of which is wrong. The intellect is necessary to discover these laws.

"Firmness" gives an inclination to hold on or to work on long lines, necessarily implying a belief in length of time, undoubtedly an eternity.

As the faculties governing or acting as agents for man's religious or æsthetic nature are classed Imitation, Benevolence, Spirituality, Hope, and Veneration.

"Imitation" has been marked with a star in the drawing, also when previously mentioned in the body of the work, to call especial attention to the fact that it was found to be necessary to explain as the function of one faculty what had formerly been allotted to three—"Human Nature," "Suavity," or "Agreeableness," and "Imitation." "Agreeableness," the desire to be or act agreeably—also, blarneying—must necessarily be caused by an appreciation of *human* nature or be the result of acting or imitation. The latter could not be performed without the ability to recognize and remember the different and peculiar manifestations belonging to human nature. This ability has been explained in the previous chapter as resulting from memory and higher comparison.

"Imitation" seems to give the appreciation of as well as a desire and ability to emulate or imitate human nature; or, in other words, that nature which is especially and solely human, as distinguished from our animal nature (explained in Chapter II).

"Benevolence" gives the feeling of pity or the inclination to exercise charity toward others. It, in front, balances self-esteem at the back, and they are necessarily counterparts in producing a harmonious character.

"Spirituality" seems to give a belief in the supernatural or the existence of something beyond man's present ken.

" Hope" seems to give a belief in the certainty of a happier, brighter state of existence, some where and some time—if not in this world, then in another. It buoys us up in the present with promises for the future.

" Veneration" gives a belief in a God or higher power, the designer and director of the universe—an all-wise and all-powerful ruler.

The relative sizes of these groups, and of the different faculties in the groups, are what make the character. These groups are rightly termed the sentiments, for they seem to have no intelligence beyond gratifying their special desires. Unless they are controlled by a well informed and harmoniously developed intellect they are apt to first sway one way and then another, as outside influences shall aid or excite the different natures. They are all selfish. The animal nature will sacrifice the rest to obtain its ends if it has the upper hand. The same is true of the social, ambitious, and the religious; and also of the intellectual. There may be great love and friendship without much ability to serve friends, great ambition without being able to discover proper means for accomplishing the desired ends, and the most devout religious feeling without the power for doing good.

" Conscientiousness " gives a sense of right and wrong, but if the intellect believes that its possesssor is in some way a superior being, and that others are inferior and born servants, he may conscientiously oppress and act toward them with the greatest tyranny. From this it will be seen that although character is of great importance, too much attention can not be given to education to see that true instead of false views are first inculcated in the mind. These first views are not often changed in after life.

It must be supposed from the general existence of harmony and order, and the apparent prevalence of a great design, that in an evenly developed character each and every one of these faculties described individually, supports and is a necessary accompaniment to every other faculty, all working together without clashing and with excellent results. But the exactly opposite must be expected when any one of them is deficient, and the greater the number of deficiences the greater the

clashing: The Social faculties rush to excess; Caution becomes fear and constantly worries; Acquisitiveness becomes
miserly; the intellect grows sharp and cynical; Combativeness continually barks and scolds; Self-esteem begets arro-
gance and tyranny; Benevolence is officious and a nuisance,
always trying to help and doing nothing but hinder; Spirituality and Hope excite to "wild-goose" chases; Veneration
turns into a fanatic; Firmness manifests itself in mulishness,
Secretiveness in trickery and deceit, and all rush pell-mell,
hither and thither, and often exhaust all of the vitality, and
sink their owner into a grave or render confinement in an
asylum necessary.

As very few characters are harmonious, one or more of the
above experiences has and does fall to the lot of each individual. The remarks on education in the following chapter
should be carefully studied, although they do not pretend to
do entire justice to that broad and important subject.

For the language of a harmonious development turn to the
biographies of those whom we consider our really great men;
although you may discover two or three, or even a single
weak faculty constantly tripping them up and causing apparent inconsistencies. For the language of a lack of harmonious
development study the lives of the most ignorant and miserable races and individuals—for the causes may all be found
in either mental or physical weaknesses or deficiencies.

In speaking of deficiencies it is not meant to imply that a
single individual of the human family is entirely deficient of the
germs of any or all of these faculties and higher natures, ready
to blossom into beauty when a few generations of favorable
circumstances shall nourish them. If they lack these human attributes or germs they can not longer be spoken of as
human, for through these higher attributes only is man more
than a brute.

If any one should feel inclined to ask why these germs
have been so long undeveloped in some while largely developed in others, I know of no other reply than to point out to
them how under favorable circumstances they were nourished
in individuals, and that it was impossible for them to be developed without favorable circumstances.

This assertion may be considered extremely radical; but I invite individual self-analysis, and then ask if it is not true that each of us finds ourself on a certain stage in life with certain abilities, and surrounded by certain circumstances, without a knowledge of the years and generations of struggling, self-sacrificing, and inurement to hardships which created the present conditions or circumstances and placed us in them. Without searching into and analyzing these pre-existing occurrences or causes, we are inclined to consider our superiority to come from some special and probably unapproachble individual or family excellence.

There can be no disputing but that favorable circumstances have produced great individual superiority, but for the capability for such superior development search has to be made back to origin; back through noble ancestry; back of blue-blood and aristocracy; back through a race of barbarians, to the primal formation, when the common parents of the whole human race first sprang upward from the dust of the earth under the inspiration of the breath of the Creator. Do any doubt this common origin? If not, how can it be doubted that intervening causes must have produced our present superiorities and inferiorities besides specially created or given excellence. What other causes are known except circumstances and the knowledge they have imparted?

You may ask " What has this to do with your subject?" Every thing when we wish to understand our relation to others; every thing, when we speak of education, for experience through circumstances has been and still is the teacher; and every thing when this fact teaches us to believe that not even the most debased are beyond the reach of the speedily-refining influences of education and favorable circumstances.

It is very probable that not an excess of one development, but the deficiency of many faculties necessary to exert a balancing or directing influence on such already strong development, produce debasement.

The causes that produced these excellencies are still existing, and are rapidly becoming known. Through the discovery of such causes, and their application, genius is becoming more and more commonly manifested.

34   KNOWLEDGE.

CHAPTER VII.

GENERAL REMARKS.

"It matters little whether a man be mathematically, or philologically,
or artistically cultivated, so he be cultivated."—*Goethe.*

In the chapter on " How History Proves Phrenology " I
have endeavored to give a description of the growth and influence of the various faculties as recorded in history, in the
three chapters just preceding merely explaining as far as
known to me the separate natural function or desire of each
nature and faculty.   Under this head I shall try to give
hints as to methods for the cultivation of the faculties and natures; to explain the probable causes which produced the
great diversities in the shapes of heads, and consequently in
character; and to treat on general laws regulating character.

When we consider the question of education it is necessary
to pay strict attention not only to one but to all of the factors
and influences which have been and are still active agents in
the progress of the human race.   The most important of
these are probably *knowledge, vitality,* and *inheritance.*   The
former is necessary to enable us to provide means for development.   The second, vitality (which is used to designate health,
strength, constitution, etc.), is indispensable to provide means
for activity, and necessarily their growth.   The third sig-
nifies the transmission or the inheritance of such development
from generation to generation.

All knowledge must have been primarily received through
the perceptives, and afterwards stored away in associated
forms, as described in Chapter III.   All conceptions, as far
as we are aware, are necessarily deductions from this knowledge by the reasoning or deducing faculties, explained in
Chapter IV as being " Calculation," " Constructiveness," " Wit,"
" Causality," and " Comparison," the activity of which faculties
was absolutely necessary for the gratification—and hence
growth—of the sentiments.

If this is the case, then it is necessary to explain a means, either natural or artificial, by which those who have not all of the perceptive and deducing faculties largely developed, have and show manifestations of a large development of the sentiments; also, to offer a reason why those with all of the perceptives and deducing faculties largely developed have not their proper share of the sentiments.

Nature seems to have practiced her usual habit of economy and forethought when she furnished storehouses for the memory of associated ideas. Man seems to have followed her example when he made letters and words to serve as signs by the use of which he could record these associated ideas, so as not to be compelled to depend entirely on his memory or again have to undergo the experiences which first led to their formation. These records are now found in our extensive libraries. After these impressions have once been received and recorded, it is easy enough to comprehend how the study of these ideas—second hand, so to speak—may feed or gratify the sentiments as easily as they would if they had been personally obtained. Deductions may also be made from such recorded ideas and develop the deducing faculties without necessary personal investigation as to their accuracy. Studying and deducing entirely from such is too widely practiced to need comment.

This has many advantages and also many disadvantages, inasmuch that unless these ideas, or knowledge (which may be either obtained from books or received from parents and instructors), be used as suggestions to be immediately proved by personal investigation as far as possible, you not only risk the danger of imbibing false ideas, which may preclude or greatly cripple further intellectual growth—as well as harmonious development of character—but render yourself a great deal more liable to forget what you have once learned. When the perceptives are used there will be as many additional aids to the memory as there are qualities or separate ideas in the formation of such knowledge. The memory of any quality may serve to recall the whole event or other particular form in which ideas and qualities have been associated.

Why people so soon forget what has been learned from books and instructors in comparison with the length of time they remember what they have learned from experience (often life-long) may be explained on this principle.

To cultivate the memory, and especially the perceptives, special attention should be paid to each of the different qualities of objects. The most attention should be particularly paid to the peculiar quality your chart will show you to be most likely not to notice.

If the perceptives are all well developed they produce a prominent ridge over the entire length of the eye, as there is an increased thickness of the skull in this region (see " sinus,"

 drawing B, and explanation, page 42). It is fair to suppose that the brain fiber should be as long here as above, if normally developed. One of the errors in the ideal head presented by Fowler, Wells & Co., is caused by the failure to make allowance for this ridge, leaving it with a slight mental deformity, as per annexed cut.

The development of the reasoning faculties depends largely upon the sentiments and upon the trade or profession which is followed (some of which employ all of them alike, and others which exercise a few of them specially). There is not one of them that can be picked out as performing a more important function than another. While great excellence in a single pursuit may be obtained with two or three of them particularly strong, the others are necessary to give business qualifications and round out the character for home or domestic responsibilities. This is very often ignored, although of the utmost importance for happiness.

Genius has been shown by one sided men, but even more often by evenly dispositioned persons. The supposition held by some that people are one sided because of their genius may justly be altered to the one that it is " because they do not possess genius enough," as Wordsworth expresses it.

" Calculation " and " Constructiveness " seem to serve the animal and social needs; " Wit," the artistic, poetic, and humerous; and " Causality " and " Comparison," the ambitious and religious or æsthetic. A fair development of each and all of them is indispensable in accurate analytical and logical reasoning.

Law, philosophy, theology, medicine, chemistry, astronomy, mechanics—all sciences, trades, and professions—are, of course, but different forms of reasoning. A knowledge of the basis of facts, the line or principle of deduction from such facts, and the results, in their relation to utility or happiness, is all that is worth knowing. There is reason to believe that any person having the different intellectual faculties well developed would be able to master or understand all these were they once systemized into a simple and comprehensive form (to which end decisive steps are now being taken). At the same time he may successfully follow a single trade or profession, for many of the principles are so closely allied that they can not fail to be valuable aids to each other. Such general study will act as a preventive against onesidedness and bigotry.

While the study of mathematics is valuable to cultivate "Calculation" and "Constructiveness," yet it might be considered an artificial means. The natural method is to continually weigh or calculate upon the food eaten; its composition and probable effects; the quantity consumed and amount of force expended; the amount of rest or sleep necessary to produce or continue certain conditions of feeling; what causes sickness, etc.; and to use the constructive power in contriving ingenious methods of economizing force, strength, etc., so as to make all ends meet with mathematical accuracy, and produce an even, harmonious state of affairs. The other reasoning faculties may be cultivated by seeking means for the gratification of the higher sentiments.

The exercise of each faculty is accompanied by a certain enjoyment and adds to our happiness. Those who have deficiencies, mental or physical, have so much less to keep them good natured. There is as much of a contrast between the lives of those who are harmoniously developed and others not so, as there is between the working of a machine which has every thing strong and taut and one that creaks and jars from loose screws and worn axles, although they may both turn out good work.

The possessing and feeling that there is a "screw loose" some where, without knowing where it is, must be the cause of a great deal of our sorrow, discontentment, and jealousy. We are apt to blame and wreak vengeance on others for what our own development produces.

To educate the deficient faculties or natures is extremely difficult. It generally requires constant and unremitting application to the very studies or exercises which are most disliked, although once developed they need only a limited amount of exercise, afford pleasure, and, with proper thought and attention and under favorable circumstances, are likely to be inherited by children.

Human nature is prone to run in ruts. The struggles necessary to cultivate another nature or set of faculties than the ones which have once gained the supremacy is noticeable in history by the revolutionary wars which invariably accompanied the progressive step of a nation, and by the private struggles of individuals in their own progress. A change of circumstances, or the reception of a new and not to be banished idea often causes such progression. When once cultivaed, the faculties not only hold their own, but can be transferred to offspring on an equal footing with the others.

This power of transmission or inheritance brings us to one of the most important, if not *the* most important subject which has yet been studied. Through the law of inheritance can be explained why there may be developments of the sentiments without the development of the intellect which was first and still remains (although artificial aids have been explained) necessary to their gratification and growth. It seems to be a law of generation that the most active and strongest faculties are inherited, with an inferior development of those which were not exercised for a length of time before conception, and probably of faculties previously over worked and exhausted.

From this fact will be seen the importance for those who are thinking of becoming parents not to fail to be careful that all of the faculties and the constitution have been properly exercised and are strong and vigorous, and under no consideration in an exhausted condition. It might be well to take special steps toward the exercise of a single weak faculty, with the view of doing as much as possible toward aiding its development in offspring (remarkable instances have been cited of the success of this venture). Care should be taken, however, not to sacrifice too much for a single faculty, there being danger of depriving others of their needed exercise.

Many books have been written on the subject of marriage adaptability and selection of mates. Some writers unqualifiedly urge people to seek their opposites, Another argues that there must be a similarity in disposition before there can be agreeable companionship, which supposition apparently has some grounds. Probably the most important guide would be to seek a harmoniously developed person, after which (as that article is very scarce), the opposites in character would likely prove most agreeable, provided the education had been similar. The children (without a thought for which no steps should be taken in this direction) would undoubtedly be better favored in this case than they could be if people with similar strong traits should unite, tending to transfer those faculties to children with ungovernable strength. Well developed, beautiful, and happy children, who have been given the opportunity to combine in themselves the strongest traits of both parents (and hence be superior in natural development to either, and should be treated accordingly) will form another bond of union. They may tend to reconcile them to each other's apparent eccentricities, and bring as much happiness to them as their natures are capable of receiving.

For, after all, what can we think or feel but what our parents thought or felt—unless we inherit from each different traits, which join in us and produce new and often more harmonious results, to be again improved by education and better opportunities.

The importance of vitality, its influence as a factor in progression, and hints toward attention to and means for increasing such, is carefully treated on in Chapter X.

CHAPTER VIII.

PHRENOLOGY EXPLAINED.

"Thou canst not wave thy staff in air, or dip thy paddle in the lake, but it carves the bow of beauty there, and the ripples in rhymes the oar forsake." . . . "Nature centers into balls, and her proud ephemerals, fast to surface and outside, scan the profile of a sphere."—*Emerson.*

I selected a spherically shaped head as a standard after first discovering, through extended and careful observations that a harmonious character was found to accompany a spherically shaped head with the axis and fullest development at the juncture of and along the region designated by the horizontal and perpendicular lines in drawing D, and the horizontal line in drawing C (hereinafter explained in detail), and that the truer the symmetry and balance forward and backward of the center-point designated in drawing D (the health-signs and constitutional strength proportionate) the more harmonious the character—as regards the proportions. The majority of heads, however, unless very small, are oblong. The supposition that the width should equal the length is merely a theory based upon the fact that the present exceedingly low rate of mortality positively proves a universally great deficit of vitality, and necessarily of the animal faculties which are indispensable for producing vitality. Also, from the idea that Nature's omnipresent love of order, symmetry, and balance, as she manifests it by continually flowing into spheres, may yet be verified in the human head. In the meantime a standard is absolutely necessary for the easy study of Phrenology, and the marking of charts by accurate measurements.

The circumference of twenty-five inches was selected with the view of having a standard size large enough to embrace all normal developments.

It may be asked, "how do you know your standard is a true one?" There is no way of proving it but for each person to investigate for themselves. It would be as impossible to prove it by words or explanations as it is why a laying hen has a red comb, and yet the farmer *knows* it is so. I am just as *positive* of the true proportions of my standard as regards symmetry and balance, and of the strong plausibility as regards breadth.

Hereafter will be given an hypothesis as a probable explanation of the physiological cause for the fullest development and axis or center-point of the head being slightly above the ear, when it is well known that the *medulla oblongata* (seated on the top of the spinal cord) is the center from which the brain radiates, and occupies a position half way between and exactly on a line with the openings of the ears—so that an instrument passed through the head through these openings would impinge its center. As this explanation would seem abstruse and uncalled for to many possible readers who have no distinct idea of Phrenology except as a sort of "bumpology," it would only be fair to endeavor to enlighten them in this particular before going further.

There is a class of readers and some teachers who are always inquiring or talking about "bumps." Probably the best way to dispose of that class is to give them the name of "Bumpologists," for Phrenology is independent of bumps.

The head may not have a bump on its surface (except the natural formations hereafter explained), but having the longest development back of the openings of the ears prove that in that region lies the most powerful and influential organs in the character. If the line diagonally backward and upward, or forward and upward, is proportionally longest, the faculties occupying those regions are the most influential; while if the line forward to the center of the lowest part of the forehead is longest, that the influence is with the intellectual development. If the head is low and broad the animal nature is the most powerful.

The Bumps

that prove such sticklers to some physiologists, and especially to a certain class of devoted "dry bone inspectors," are all natural formations of the skull (unless where the skull is worn by abnormal activity leaving different thicknesses, as below noticed). They occur in every head (children under twelve, excepted) and hence are easily allowed for.

These formations are the *occipital protuberance,* a bony projection found in the lowest part of the back head, and which is used for the attachment to the skull of the strong muscles of the body; the *superciliary ridge,* a bony ridge under the eyebrows and above the nose; the *frontal sinus,* a cavity between the two plates of the skull under this ridge; the *sutures* of the skull, or the seams joining the different plates of the skull, and at which seams there is often deposited a surplus of bony material, causing irregularities; and a bony process immediately behind the ear, which is hardly worth naming as it lies inside of all of the places marked in the drawing as representing the location of any faculty.

The activity and growth of the brain no more changes the natural formation or shape of the bone that incases it than the oyster does that of its shell in the process of growth. The organs merely extending the case—bony projections, cavities, and all as they were first made—although they may wear different parts thin as well as extend them. An examination of a large collection of untenanted skulls proved to me, and will prove to others if they honestly desire to determine, that in every instance where the skull was worn thin, it was also broadened or extended in that region. This thinness probably resulted from an abnormal activity, the chemical action of the blood dissolving the bone more rapidly than it could reconstruct it.

Deficiencies of certain faculties do cause depressions and leave rounded protuberances; but these are not likely to assume the appearance of bumps, and especially not the pointed bumps resulting from the contusion of the head with hard substances. They also differ greatly in the fact that developments are found to exist in both hemispheres of the brain in like position. Bumps, besides being pointed, have no corresponding elevation on the opposite side, and would have to be exceedingly large to make a difference in sizes.

That much for "bumps," and now for the hypothesis explaining why the axis or fullest development should be at the point hereinafter designated. This is followed by a detailed description of how to study Phrenology and mark a chart, which will probably leave with many of those who will devote the necessary time to its study and comprehension, the first clear ideas they ever possessed of the true principles of Phrenology.

Hypothesis.

If the brain radiates from the *medulla oblongata*, which is directly on a line with the openings of the ears, a reason must be given why the axis or center of the sphere of the head has been located at a point above the ear in the drawings. This reason can be found in the fact that a portion of the space in the skull must be allotted to the brain governing the senses. It can not be otherwise than that the brain governing the senses—which are so closely allied to mere physical existence, and their strength and activity absolutely necessary for the gratification of the desires—must have a seat nearest and surrounding the brain center. Its necessary size, judging by the number and importance of the functions it directs, must cause the rest of the brain to be forced upward before it has room to spread or ramify in each direction from a common center point. The height of this point is probably regulated by the breadth of the head (hereinafter explained), as the senses (except sight) are most essential to the animal nature.

Detailed Explanation.

The following description has been arranged as an aid to students, as well as to show that the adoption of a standard has almost reduced Phrenology to a mathematical science. There is need for very little guess work when a pair of calipers (specially constructed for the purpose) and a tape-measure can be obtained, and no careful Phrenologist will neglect their use.

In making examinations first take a tape measurement around the head parallel with the lowest part of the forehead (see horizontal line in drawing C, next page). This measurement determines the circumference by which "SIZE" is marked in the chart—always making allowance for size of the

DRAWING C.

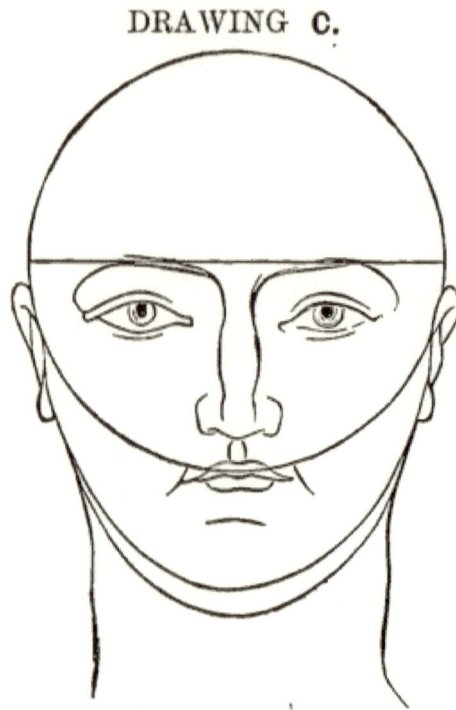

superciliary ridge and probable thickness of the skull, from the apparent amount of bony material in the general make up—to be judged by the size of the bones and the prominence of the *occipital protuberance.*

Another method of ascertaining the relative thickness of the skull is to lay the hand on a person's head while he is speaking—if the skull is very thin vibrations will be distinctly felt.

The development of the animal group is then ascertained by taking a caliper measurement of the breadth of the head above the ears at the point where the shortest line joins the longest or horizontal line (the ʌxɪs) in drawing D, next page. The relative size of each faculty is to be determined as hereinafter described.

The length of the head is caused by the intellectual group forward and the social group backward of the center point above mentioned. To ascertain their size the entire length must first be determined with the calipers. This can be done by placing the opposite ends of the calipers at the points designated by the two ends of the horizontal line in drawing D. Half of this length shows the size of either if they are balanced—by no means always the case, one of these groups often being several sizes larger than the other. This difference in relative length can be determined by finding the distances from the opening of the ear to each of the points before men-

DRAWING D.

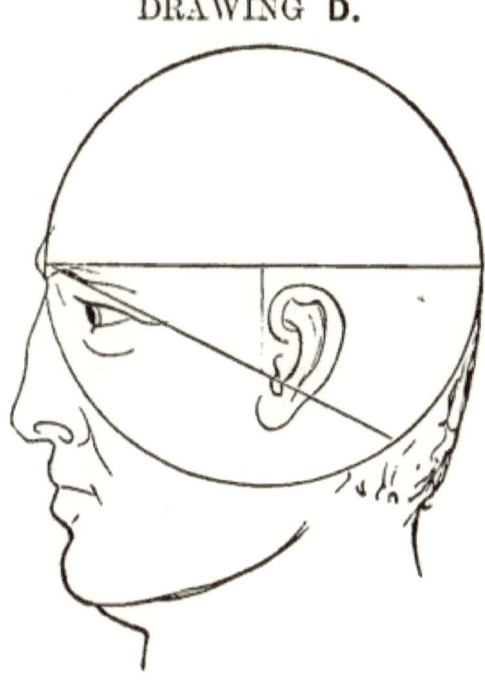

tioned, and comparing them; or by measuring from the center point to these extremities. The latter requires the exercise of considerable care to keep the end of the calipers directly on the point, while the same end can be arrived at more easily by the other method.

After the number of sizes in the difference of length from this center point are found (which can be judged by the eye) they are to be added to or subtracted from one-half of the entire length before determined.

The development of the ambitious and the religious or æsthetic groups are slightly more difficult to determine.

By taking a tape measurement from the opening of one ear directly over the head to the opening of the other ear the general fullness of the top-head is ascertained. The greatest part of this fullness may be caused by either the upper groups or the lower group of faculties, according to their size. For instance, a narrow head might measure the same by this measurement as a broad head (one having height and the other breadth), and still represent entirely different characters.

To avoid a mistake in this direction the breadth of the head should be taken into consideration, and one-half of an inch of fullness allowed for one-third of an inch (a size) in width, all of which will be carefully explained hereafter.

In the standard (see short perpendicular line, above figure)

I have estimated one-fourth of the entire diameter (or two inches for a head twenty-five inches in circumference and eight inches in diameter—the standard size) for the distance from the brain center to the radiating point above the brain governing the senses. This one-fourth, if the head was eight inches wide, would give four inches, two inches on each side. This, added to the eight inches of breadth, would give a circumference of twelve inches over the top from ear opening to ear opening, independent of any of the higher faculties, which are all above the horizontal line in the drawings. A decrease in breadth, it is fair to suppose, must necessarily be followed by a proportionate decrease in the height of the above mentioned brain. As two is one-fourth of eight, for every inch less in width there is one-fourth of an inch less in height on each side. This takes an inch and a half from the before mentioned circumference for every inch less of width, and still leaves a balance of the different groups similar to the proportions in the standard—only, a few sizes smaller.

The sizes are arranged according to the circumference, No. 8 representing the standard. As the diameter is about one-third of the circumference (without going further into fractions), the sizes determined by length and breadth decrease one-third of an inch to every inch of circumference. In comparing the relative developments backward and forward of the center point, one-sixth of an inch is a size.

Chart No.	Circumference.	Length.	Width.	Circumference over top of head from ear-opening to ear-opening.
8	25 in.	8	8	$16\frac{1}{2}$
7	24 in.	$7\frac{2}{3}$	$7\frac{2}{3}$	16
6	23 in.	$7\frac{1}{3}$	$7\frac{1}{3}$	$15\frac{1}{2}$
5	22 in.	7	7	15
4	21 in.	$6\frac{2}{3}$	$6\frac{2}{3}$	$14\frac{1}{2}$
3	20 in.	$6\frac{1}{3}$	$6\frac{1}{3}$	14
2	19 in.	6	6	$13\frac{1}{2}$
1	18 in.	$5\frac{2}{3}$	$5\frac{2}{3}$	13
0	17 in.	$5\frac{1}{3}$	$5\frac{1}{3}$	$12\frac{1}{2}$

This table was prepared to show the relative measurements necessary to a harmonious development or complete balance all around, supposing the rest of the head to be symmetrical. If it is not symmetrical, the eye will serve as one guide and the hands as another, to determine what faculties fail to come up to the proportions. But for a far more reliable method of determining the comparitive size of the ambitious and the religious sentiments, as well as the size of the faculties located along different lines, as hereafter explained, the calipers should be used.

To determine the relative size of the ambitious and religious group (after their general size has been determined by the circumference over the top head, etc., as before described), one of the ends of the calipers should be held in place at the point of juncture of the longest and shortest line, designated in drawing D. The other end is then carefully circled from the top point (designated by the star point in drawing B, page vi) backward and forward, exactly in the center of the head as regards width, over the region occupied by the faculties causing those sentiments, as seen in the drawings. It may be extended down to the *frontal sinus* in front and to the *occipital protuberance* behind—*i. e.*, where the neck joins the skull—to find the comparative sizes of the faculties located along that entire line. By holding one end carefully at the top point before alluded to, and circling the lower end around one side or hemisphere, the comparative size of that range of organs may be determined. Another range of faculties can be examined by placing one end of the calipers at the point designated by the back end of the horizontal line in drawing D, and circling the other end over the top head.

By comparing the widths of the head where the different faculties giving the animal nature are located, with the width at the part designated as the center point, which should be the most extended, their relative influence can be detected.

After all these measurements have been taken, and the chart marked accordingly, a person with average abilities can estimate the size of the remaining faculties pretty correctly by an off-hand judgment.

It must be remembered that although circumference is a measure of power if all other conditions are equal, those other conditions are so extremely important that frequently such ceases to indicate power. A full side and back head may cause large circumference, and at the same time fail to be accompanied by the intellectual power belonging to a head a size smaller, if the intellectual development be longer and more harmonious in the latter than in the former. If a good intellect is not strongly backed up by the other natures, it is not likely to show brilliant manifestations—on the principle that although there may be power, it will not be displayed without the prompting inspiration given by the sentiments.

By careful study of the principles set forth in this chapter, a person with good mathematical ability, by the use of a tape measure and calipers,* if careful may learn to mark the chart in the following chapter with considerable accuracy.

To be able to delineate character is far more difficult. In delineation it is not the strength of the faculties that is told, but the actions which will result from the varied influence upon each other of both strong and weak faculties, under different circumstances.

Small faculties—Self-esteem, for instance—are continually struggling for their share of power, and occasionally make themselves felt, like a small boy trying to maintain his rights against older ones; but their struggles are soon quieted. In moments of great importance they are completely sacrificed.

Probably the surest method for studying Phrenology is to first get a chart of your head marked according to the herein presented standard (and a delineation by a reliable Phrenologist, if obtainable), and continually seek to explain your own actions as resulting from the combined influence of the intellect and the sentiments, consulting a reliable book of reference (which I have endeavored to make of this) until you are perfectly familiar with the separate duty or function of each faculty. If a friend has a chart which you are allowed to consult, it will, of course, give you two subjects for study instead of one. Better still, if a class or society is formed and measuring instruments procured, its different members can be studied until the eye is trained—then the world full of people is your school-room.

---

* If the author is addressed through the publishers he will endeavor to secure for students both calipers and tape measures at the lowest price.

CHAPTER IX.

CHART—EXPLANATION.

"I saw men go up and down, in the country and the town, with this tablet on their neck—judgment and a judge we seek."—*Emerson.*

The chart on the last two pages of this chapter will be found to be an honest judge, marked—not by guess work but—by actual measurements, as described in the preceding chapter, and "*figures won't lie.*"

The first three sizes (0, 1, 2) are for children's heads, while the remaining sizes are for adults'. Special faculties in children's heads may range with adults', and *vice versa.*

The SIZE is gauged by the circumference (see page 43), after allowance has been made for skull (see page 44).

QUALITY is estimated by the smoothness of the skin, fineness of the hair, and general physical symmetry.

TEXTURE is marked according to the apparent compactness of the tissue and muscles. There is a necessary relation between brain texture and physical texture.

VITALITY is judged by breadth of head, weight, health, and apparent constitutional strength, giving power of endurance.

[The above points and the comparative strength of the different groups or natures are first marked as a general *outline* of the character, after which the strength of each faculty is noted.]

For explanations of natures and separate faculties carefully study Chapters II, IV, V, and VI.

A certain constitution or amount of vitality is bequeathed to each with birth. How much advancement such birthright will enable us to make and what efforts to undergo in life there is probably no means of ascertaining. It may be affirmed, though, that even the weakest constitution is asure to respond to and improve under intelligent and scientific care and attention, if you understand your weakest points. These are marked in chart according to the following health signs;

The health signs are as follows :

Lungs.—The nostrils are not only provided with a very fine sieve of hair to prevent dirt from entering into the lungs, but also are so arranged that the temperature of the air inhaled is modified in its passage through them. If they are narrow and contracted, it is proof that the breathing has been done mostly through the mouth. This not only exposes the lungs to possible injury from floating particles of dirt and corruption, but also brings them into almost direct contact with the air, which is extremely dangerous in cold weather. When an organ adapted for a special purpose is not so used, bad results are sure to be produced. Breathing should be done entirely throuh the nostrils while exercising to broaden them.

Blood.—Rosy lips and cheeks, and clearness of complexion showthe condition of the blood. This is an important agent in development. Careful habits, exercise, and particular attention to the diet is necessary to regulate and purify it.

Heart—A broad, full chin has been found to accompany a sound heart and strong pulse. Very careful exercise is necessary for its cultivation, if weak.

Digestion.—Full cheeks are caused by a secretion of saliva therein, which is a necessary aid in digestion (see pages 58, 59). Carefully chewing each mouthful of food, and eating proper food (see three last pages of chapter X) will tend to increase the secretion of saliva, and hence fill out the cheek. This is as important to beauty as it is to excellent health.

Breathing power.—High and broad cheek bones accompany a full, deep chest, giving strong breathing power. This can be cultivated by habitually inflating the lungs to their utmost depth or capacity.

MALE vs. FEMALE.—Differing from most Phrenologists, and from many eminent thinkers, I see no reason for believing that there *should* be any *mental* difference between man and woman, and hence mark the charts for both by the same standard.

Realizing the bulk of prejudice against this side of the question it is, of course, worse than useless to stop and argue it in this work. At the same time a few words in defense of my position seem necessary. The following points may afford food for thought for those who have not had time to study the question, or do not possess incurable prejudices.

If any one claims that the male sex does to-day (and has as

far back as history records) average a great intellectual and physical superiority over the female sex, and that the greatest genius yet displayed has been by man, it can not be denied. If they assert that because this has been so—it is therefore a proper and unalterable condition—the justice of such a supposition may be as justly ridiculed as it would be if made in regard to slave holding, or of might making right. These have been and are gradually being rejected, as disgusting relics of barbaric ages.

The difference in sex has been used as the basis of long-winded arguments by numerous learned doctors. They have endeavored to prove that such difference necessitated a physical inferiority as regards strength and endurance, and they may be right. It would be well for them, however, to give an explanation for the numerous instances in which women have shown wonderful strength and power of endurance—if it is a law of nature that they can not possess it.

On the other hand, is there no plausibility in the theory that if one sex has been prevented—either by might or from the bias resulting from false ideas or customs—from securing high general culture, they would grow weaker, and that such weakness (especially physical) would most likely fall to the child that inherited the sex. Also, that the false ideas and education which produced such differences may still still be actively at work in perpetuating them.

That the inherited difference in ability is not so great as might be supposed is evident from the almost equal contests, both muscular and mental, between children up to the age when girls are first taught that it is unlady-like to romp out of doors, and she begins to shrink from the name of "tom-boy," and when boys are turned out of the house or set to manual work. In seminaries where they have been on the same footing, women have held their own. If they have failed to prove equal in the long run—inheritance, education, and opportunities—all alterable—are probable causes.

It is not surroundings, but thought which causes development, and the love of home and children should be as influential in inspiring man in his duties as it is to woman.

[SEE TABLE ON PAGE 46.]

No......................................	0	1	2	3	4	5	6	7	8
CIRCUMFERENCE [inches].........	17	18	19	20	21	22	23	24	25
1. SIZE									
2. QUALITY...........................									
3. TEXTURE....................									
4. VITALITY...									
5. ANIMAL NATURE............									
6. SOCIAL NATURE.................									
7. AMBITIOUS NATURE............									
8. RELIGIOUS NATURE.............									
9. INTELLECTUAL NATURE........									
10. INDIVIDUALITY............									
11. FORM...............									
12. Size................................									
13. Weight...........................									
14. Color............									
15. Order..............................									
16. EVENTUALITY									
17. Locality............									
18. Time........... ....;.....									
19. Tune..............................									
20. Language...........									
21. CALCULATION...........									
22. Constructiveness..									
23. Wit...............									
24. Causality									
25. Comparison......									

[SEE TABLE ON PAGE 46.]

No	0	1	2	3	4	5	6	7	8
CIRCUMFERENCE [inches]	17	18	19	20	21	22	23	24	25
26. VITATIVENESS									
27. Alimentiveness									
28. Destructiveness									
29. Combativeness									
30. Alimentiveness									
31. CONJUGALITY									
32. Philoprogenitiveness									
33. Friendship									
34. Adhesiveness									
35. Inhabitativeness									
36. CONTINUITY									
37. Self-esteem									
38. Approbativeness									
39. Conscientiousness									
40. Firmness									
41. IMITATION									
42. Benevolence									
43. Spirituality									
44. Hope									
45. Veneration									
46. *Lungs*									
47. *Blood*									
48. *Heart*									
49. *Digestion*									
50. *Breathing Power*									

CHAPTER X.

CHARACTER vs. HEALTH—HEALTH vs. FOOD.

"In college I was taught all about the motions of the planets, as carefully as though they would have been in danger of getting off the track if I had not known how to trace their orbits ; but about the conditions indispensable to the healthful functions of my own body I was left in profound ignorance."—*Horace Mann.*

No treatise on mental science is complete without due notice being taken of the influence of health in the manifestation of character and ability.

The most powerful steam engine or magnificent piece of mechanism ever constructed is valueless unless due provision has been made to furnish the proper motive or sustaining power to enable it to display the splendid effects of its excellent construction. The same is undeniably true of the most magnificent human attributes that ever gave harmonious shape to a head.

A ten-horse power engine with a proper sized boiler will do as good if not better work than a twenty-horse power engine with a boiler only large enough for a ten-horse power engine. The same relation exists between the head and body as between the engine and boiler in this respect; but materially differing in the fact that the engine has not the power to drain and weaken the boiler for its own activity which the brain has over the body. We all laugh at the ignorance of the man in the fable who killed the goose that laid the golden egg. At the same time the majority of us are acting on the same principle in our negligent ignorance in regard to physical care and attention.

What an old subject this is! Why, it might be just to exhort you to respect and venerate it from its very age, as many do for old-time customs and institutions which are really useless and obsolete as far as real benefit is concerned. The most irreverent will probably not dare to affirm as much for this subject. After all, it is not length of time that will bring the corn crop to a harvest of golden ears, as much as it is the necessary care and attention accompanied by favorable weather or circumstances. Care and attention is what this subject has not had.

Let us first endeavor to get a clear idea of what health or vitality really is. Nine out of ten will consider themselves perfectly healthy if they do not have to stay in bed and be nursed. Many will consider themselves healthy if they can keep going with the occasional aid of medicine or stimulants, or both. But is this health? If not, "how can we determine what health is?" may be justly asked.

While I should by far prefer to be given "some thing easy," consistency compels me to wrestle with this problem.

There seems to be no single means of determining the true condition of health. The doctor looks at your tongue, and the phrenologist at the health signs in the face, and often closely approximate the true condition, but not always. The old adage about appearances being some times deceitful holds as true in regard to health as it does in regard to character judged by physiognomy. For an additional aid to determine health, the manifestations must be studied for facts to form a basis from which further deductions can be made and a hypothesis formed. A hypothesis has been truthfully asserted to be to the discovery of new truths what scaffolding is to a house—i. e., absolutely necessary to its formation, but merely unnecessary lumber afterwards.

It is said of a boy that unless he jumps over every post, slams every gate, jerks every pump-handle, and throws a stone or clod of dirt at every inoffensive looking dog he meets on his way to school, there is assuredly something the matter with him. This is another way of saying that certain manifestations mean health, and health means certain manifestations, in boys. There is no reason to believe that the same rule does not embrace both small boys and large boys, called men, for where is there one who is fully developed.

Judging from manifestations it may be broadly affirmed that a sound constitution and good health will not only cause great activity, but will sustain and develop a large head. There appears no reason to believe that growth* and activity of brain will cease till death if these points are strong (supposing the apex of human excellence not to have been previously arrived at), unless the intellect has been biased by erroneous ideas, incompatible with harmonious growth (commented on in Chapter VII). In this case the excess of vitality is sure to cause an excessive exercise of the faculties already developed —bound to end in some kind of sickness and disease, and often to cause insanity as a result of abnormal activity.

If old age brings or has brought with it no such growth or manifestations, the above principles must explain the cause to be a deficiency of vitality. Whether that is mostly due from inheritence, or from your own ignorance and negligence, all must determine for themselves, although it may be positively affirmed that all three were factors.

Many may think themselves healthy because they have been enabled to jog along comfortably in an accustomed path, but a change of circumstances (always liable to occur from accidents or other causes), bringing with it prostration, as it so often does, may apprise them of how faint a support they had been leaning on. They may get a sort of an idea of their true weakness by comparing the puny expenditure of force required in their small sphere of usefulness with that of many others, whose activity is enormous. The sole explanation yet offered for this difference is superiority in health and constitution, which are supposed to be both embraced in the word VITALITY.

The necessity of a certain amount of exercise for the continuance of health is almost universally acknowledged. A more important point than exercise, and without attention to which exercise is more hurtful than beneficial, has been generally overlooked. This is the proper care and attention to the nutritive properties contained in the food eaten, and the action of the digestive acids on these properties in the forms they assume in the different articles of food.

---

* A personal instance has been given me of the head increasing over an inch in circumference between the ages of twenty-seven and seventy.

Of course, if any of my readers are possessed of the inexplicable belief that unaided instinct is a safe guide as to what we should eat, the following pages will have no interest to them. If they have a belief in it as a reliable guide, however, I beg them to explain why instinct has made such an apparently botched job of the affair as must have been necessary to leave us in our present half developed condition with an average length of life but slightly exceeding thirty years. The lives of brutes have been estimated to be about five times that of man by a comparison of the length of existence after maturity with the time required to mature.

What is *instinct* any way, that it should be an absolutely reliable guide? It is explained as a blind consciousness directing us—but that leaves us where it found us as regards what it really is, as it hints at no cause or further explanation of this power. If it is a directing power it must be a process of reasoning, for reason alone directs. Then we must seek an explanation (for to seek to explain or to study is the only exit out of ignorance and superstition) why it differs in its incomprehensibly quick, fine, and insensible action (so rapid, so smooth, as to leave only the impression after the work is done) from the slow careful, labored efforts usually understood to be reasoning.

For explanation it is necessary to revert back to the principle commented on in Chapter VIII, noted in the necessary struggling for development, and the ease and pleasure with which such is afterward exercised, and the law of inheritance, with the additional application of the principle emphasized in the well known adage: "practice makes perfect." We can then realize that a habit or custom practiced by a parent or parents through one or more generations, might be performed by an offspring unconsciously and with wonderful accuracy. This reasoning allows us to appreciate the strong plausibility of the definition presented by one of our greatest modern naturalists, that instinct results from inherited development first cultivated by our parents.

If this definition is true it will be seen that to find out how reliable your instinct may be a search will have to be made

back through a few generations of ancestors to see that they
have not cultivated some abnormal and injurious habit of eating which they did not inherit, or even acquire early enough
in life to have a biasing influence on their maturement; but
soon enough to transfer to you as an instinct a desire for some
thing which may be so injurious as to make your whole life
miserable.   Such search would be far more difficult than to
study and prove the truth of the laws and facts which I have
hereinafter set forth.

If the truth were summed up it would probably show that
instinct has been used as a scape-goat by a class of people who
have never thought much of the subject, and endeavored to
hide their ignorance.

It is a well known fact in regard to firing and heating that
certain kinds of fuel are differently affected in combustion,
producing various effects, as regards the time consumed in
decomposition and the intensity of heat produced, different
kinds of fuel being most valuable for different or peculiar purposes.   All this is also true in regard to the fuel or food fed
into the human furnace.

Probably the most easily digested article of food in common
use is sugar, into which starch is first converted by the chemical action of the saliva (secreted in the cheeks) in the process
of digestion.   The same material found in the forms of
starch and sugar—which is pure carbon or heating material—when in the form of fat or grease, partially if not
wholly resists the action of such siliva.   It has to pass in its
natural form through the stomach, until it reaches what is
known as the "second stomach."   Here it is acted upon by
the *pancreatic juices,* and then digested, unless forced through
the system too rapidly by its own weight or the weight of
other articles of food, which is probably often the case.

That much of the food eaten by many persons is not digested is self-evident from the fact that if it were all digested
and assimilated every hearty eater would become exceedingly
fleshy and corpulent—unless the supply is counterbalanced by
the wastes, not liable unless engaged in exceedingly active
mental or physical exercise.   Many hearty eaters neither
work hard nor increase in flesh.

It may be seen that there are two aids to digestion (the saliva and pancreatic juices). They are both important agents in the digestion of different articles of food.

From the nature of greasy foods it seems that they are better adapted (if not in too large pieces) to pass easily through the system to the second stomach than starchy articles. The latter may prove to be irritating to the delicate membranes of the stomach unless thoroughly saturated by the saliva—in which latter condition they are more rapidly digested than greasy foods can possibly be, as is apparent.

Thus habits which tend to exhaust the saliva necessary for the digestion (as tobacco chewing, and even gum chewing, if the saliva secreted is not exceedingly abundant), may possibly, on the above principle, indirectly produce very dangerous results. This may also hold true when the food is swallowed too hastily or washed down by water, either from a cup or from being previously mixed with the food in such proportions as not to need the motion of the jaws (necessary to cause an abundant flow of saliva, which also retains it in the mouth and gives the saliva time for action), as it is in soups and mushes. These should not be eaten except with some hard substances— dry bread or crusts. Carlyle probably suffered with the dyspepsia not only while *but* from eating oat-meal and milk, while others were more fortunate.

The table below shows the various nutritive properties of some of our most common articles of food. It is generally agreed upon by those who have experimented that the wheat grain (Graham flour) is the best proportioned (as well as one of the most easily digested—as are all flours) food for general health, and that it will sustain a great amount of physical and mental exertion. This fact renders it very valuable as a standard by which to judge the value of the other articles of food. It is evident that the food should be selected according to the demands and wastes (as well as to the power for digesting). The physical man should never be slighted.

As to pepper, vinegar, tobacco, and all fermented liquids or foods which are so composed as to seem naturally repugnant either in taste or smell, although a desire for such may be cultivated, they should be avoided if on no other grounds than that they may destroy the relish for plain, substantial foods (which can be and are made sweet and appetizing to the normal palate). It has been ascertained, however, that all of them are otherwise more or less injurious. Fermentation in liquids is probably analogous to decay and rottenness in solids.

There is hardly any of the modes of preparing white flour which are not applicable to Graham flour. A meal on bread and butter, if pure Graham is used, is equivalent to a hearty and subsantial repast. If white flour is used it is a trashy (in spite of being æsthetic) one, not only being devoid of brain and muscle making elements, but also tending to produce biliousness, constipation, and other complaints, both through its superabundance of saccharine matter and its absence of waste particles necessary to keep the system clean and active.

Coffee and tea are apt to cause constipation and nervousness. An excellent substitute is hot water with milk and sugar.

ARTICLES OF FOOD.	Heat & fat.	Muscle-making	Brain & bone	Water & waste
Graham flour......................	69.8	15.0	1.6	13.6
White flour........................	100.0	....	....	....
Oats..............................	66.4	17.0	3.0	13.6
Rye..............................	71.5	13.8	1.7	13.0
Barley............................	69.5	17.0	3.5	10.0
Northern corn	73.0	12.0	1.0	14.0
Southern corn....................	45.0	35.0	4.0	16.0
Buckwheat........................	75.4	8.6	1.8	14.2
Beans............................	57.7	24.0	3.5	14.8
Peas	60.0	23.4	2.5	14.1
Rice	79.5	6.5	.5	13.5
Potatoes	22.5	1.4	.9	75.2
Sweet Potatoes....................	26.5	1.5	2.9	59.1
Turnips...........	4.0	1.1	.5	94.4
Cabbage	5.0	4.0	1.0	90.0
Parsnips.........................	7.0	1.2	1.0	90.8
Carrots	6.6	.6	1.0	91.8
Apples...........................	10.0	5.0	1.0	84.0
Eggs	29.0	23.6	.5	33.0
Cheese	19.0	65.0	7.0	9.0
Butter............................	100.0	....	....	....
Cow-milk.........................	8.0	5.0	1.0	86.0
Human-milk	7.0	3.0	.5	89.5
Oysters..	....	10.0	2.0	88.0
Fresh Fish (average).	.5	17.0	5.0	77.5
Mutton (lean)	40.0	12.5	3.5	44.0
Beef "	30.0	15.0	5.0	50.0
Pork "	50.0	10.0	1.5	38.5
Chicken	25.0	20.0	4.5	50.5

Beer and alcoholic liquors. .. ..Fat and heat making.

PUBLICATIONS

OF

ROBERT CLARKE & CO.,

CINCINNATI, O.

HISTORICAL AND MISCELLANEOUS.

ALZOG (John D. D.) A Manual of Universal Church History. Translated by Rev. T. J. Pabisch and Rev. T. S. Byrne. 3 vols. 8vo. 15 00

ANDERSON (E. L.) Six Weeks in Norway. 18mo. 1 00

ANDRE (Major). The Cow Chase; an Heroick Poem. 8vo. Paper 75

ANTRIM (J.) The History of Champaign and Logan Counties, Ohio, from their First Settlement. 12mo. 1 50

BALLARD (Julia P.) Insect Lives; or, Born in Prison. Illustrated. Sq. 12mo. 1 00

BASSLER (S. S.) The Weather. A Practical Guide to its Changes. 8vo. Paper. 25

BELL (Thomas J.) History of the Cincinnati Water Works. Plates. 8vo. 75

BENNER (S.) Prophecies of Future Ups and Downs in Prices: What Years to Make Money in Pig Iron, Hogs, Corn, and Provisions. 3d ed. 24mo. 1 00

BIBLE IN THE PUBLIC SCHOOLS. Records. Arguments, etc., in the Case of Minor vs. Board of Education or Cincinnati. 8vo. 2 00
Arguments in Favor of the Use of the Bible. Separate. Paper, 50
Arguments Against the Use of the Bible. Separate. Paper, 50

BIBLIOTHECA AMERICANA. 1883. Being a priced Catalogue of a large Collection (nearly 7,000 items) of Books and Pamphlets relating to America. 8vo. 312 pages. Paper. 50c.; Cloth, 1 00

BIDDLE (Horace P.) Elements of Knowledge. 12mo. 1 00

BIDDLE (Horace P.) Prose Miscellanies. 12mo. 1 00

BOUQUET (H.) The Expedition of, against the Ohio Indians in 1764, etc. With Preface by Francis Parkman, Jr. 8vo. $3.00. Large paper 6 00

BOYLAND (G. H., M.D.) Six Months Under the Red Cross with the French Army in the Franco-Prussian War. 12mo. 1 50

BRUNNER (A. A.) Elementary and Pronouncing French Reader. 18mo. 60

BRUNNER (A. A.) The Gender of French Verbs Simplified. 18mo. 25

BURT (Rev. N. C., D.D.) The Far East; or Letters from Egypt, Palestine, etc. 12mo. 1 75

BUTTERFIELD (C. W.) The Washington-Crawford Letters; being

the Correspondence between George Washington and William Crawford, concerning Western Lands. 8vo.   1 00

BUTTERFIELD (C. W.) The Discovery of the Northwest in 1634, by John Nicolet, with a Sketch of his Life. 12mo.   1 00

CLARK (Col. George Rogers). Sketches of his Campaign in the Illinois in 1778-9. With an Introduction by Hon Henry Pirtle, and an Appendix. 8vo. $2 00. Large paper,   4 00

COFFIN (Levi.) The Reminiscences of Levi Coffin, the Reputed President of the Underground Railroad. A Brief History of the Labors of a Lifetime in behalf of the Slave. With Stories of Fugitive Slaves, etc., etc. 12mo.   2 00

COLLIER (Peter). Sorghum: its Culture and Manufacture Economically Considered, and as a Source of Sugar, Syrup and Fodder. Illustrated. 8vo.   3 00

CONSTITUTION OF THE UNITED STATES, ETC. The Declaration of Independence, July 4, 1776; the Articles of Confederation, July 9, 1778; the Constitution of the United States, September 17, 1787; the Fifteen Amendment to the Constitution, and Index; Washington's Farewell Address, September 7, 1796. 8vo. Paper.   25

CORNWELL (H G.) Consultation Chart of the Eye-Symptoms and Eye-Complications of General Disease. 14 x 20 inches. Mounted on Roller.   50

CRAIG (N. B.) The Olden Time. A Monthly Publication, devoted to the Preservation of Documents of Early History, etc. Originally Published at Pittsburg, in 1846-47. 2 vols. 8vo.   10 00

DRAKE (D.) Pioneer Life in Kentucky. Edited, with Notes and a Biographical Sketch by his Son, Hon. Chas. D. Drake. 8vo. $3 00. Large paper.   6 00

DUBREUIL (A.) Vineyard Culture Improved and Cheapened. Edited by Dr. J. A. Warder. 12mo.   2 00

ELLARD (Virginia G.) Grandma's Christmas Day. Illus. Sq. 12mo.   1 00

EVERTS (Orpheus). What Shall We Do With the Drunkard? A Rational View of the Use of Brain Stimulants. 8vo. Paper.   50

FAMILY EXPENSE BOOK. A Printed Account Book, with Appropriate Columns and Headings, for keeping a Complete Record of Family Expenses. 12mo.   50

FINLEY (I. J.) and PUTNAM (R.) Pioneer Record and Reminiscences of the Early Settlers and Settlement of Ross County, Ohio. 8vo.   2 50

FLETCHER (Wm. B., M.D.) Cholera: its Characteristics, History, Treatment, etc. 8vo. Paper.   1 00

FORCE (M. F.) Essays Pre-Historic Man—Darwinism and Deity—The Mound Builders. 8vo. Paper.

FORCE (M. F.) Some Early Notices of the Indians of Ohio. To What Race did the Mound Builders Belong? 8vo. Paper.   50

FREEMAN (Ellen). Manual of the French Verb, to accompany every French Course. 16mo. Paper.   25

GALLAGHER (Wm. D.) Miami Woods, A Golden Wedding, and
other Poems. 12mo.   2 00
GRIMKE (F.) Considerations on the Nature and Tendency of
Free Institutions. 8vo.   2 50
GRISWOLD (W.) Kansas: Her Resources and Developments; or,
the Kansas Pilot. 8vo. Paper.   50
HALL (James). Legends of the West. Sketches illustrative of
the Habits, Occupations, Privations, Adventures, and Sports
of the Pioneers of the West. 12mo.   2 00
HALL (James). Romance of Western History; or, Sketches of
History, Life, and Manners in the West. 12mo.   2 00
HANOVER (M. D.) A Practical Treatise on the Law of Horses,
embracing the Law of Bargain, Sale, and Warranty of Horses
and other Live Stock; the Rule as to Unsoundness and Vice,
and the Responsibility of the Proprietors of Livery, Auction,
and Sale Stables, Inn-keepers, Veterinary Surgeons, and Far-
riers, Carriers, etc. 8vo.   4 00
HART (J. M.) A Syllabus of Anglo-Saxon Literature. 8vo.
Paper.   50
HASSAUREK (F.) The Secret of the Andes. A Romance.
12mo.   1 50
THE SAME, in German. 8vo. Paper, 50c.; cloth,   1 00
HASSAUREK (F.) Four Years Among Spanish Americans. Third
Edition. 12mo.   1 50
HATCH (Col. W. S.) A Chapter in the History of the War of
1812, in the Northwest, embracing the Surrender of the
Northwestern Army and Fort, at Detroit, August 16, 1813, etc.
18mo.   1 25
HAYES (Rutherford B.) The Life, Public Services, and Select
Speeches of. Edited by J. Q. Howard. 12mo. Paper, 75c.;
Cloth.   1 25
HAZEN (Gen. W. B.) Our Barren Lands. The Interior of the
United States, West of the One-Hundredth Meridian, and
East of the Sierra Nevada. 8vo. Paper.   50
HENSHALL (Dr. James A.) Book of the Black Bass; comprising
its complete Scientific and Life History, together with a Prac-
tical Treatise on Angling and Fly Fishing, and a full de-
scription of Tools, Tackle, and Implements. Illustrated.
12mo.   3 00
HORTON (S. Dana). Silver and Gold, and their Relation to the
Problem of Resumption. 8vo.   1 50
HORTON (S. Dana). The Monetary Situation. 8vo. Paper.   50
HOUGH (Franklin B.) Elements of Forestry. Designed to afford
Information concerning the Planting and Care of Forest Trees
for Ornament and Profit; and giving Suggestions upon the
Creation and Care of Woodlands, with the view of securing
the greatest benefit for the longest time. Particularly adapted
to the wants and conditions of the United States. Illus-
trated. 12mo.   2 00
HOUSEKEEPING IN THE BLUE GRASS. A New and Practical Cook
Book. By Ladies of the Presbyterian Church, Paris, Ky.
12mo. 13th thousand.   1 50
HOVEY (Horace C.) Celebrated American Caverns, especially

Mammoth, Wyandot, and Luray; together with Historical, Scientific, and Descriptive Notices of Caves and Grottoes in Other Lands. Maps and Illustrations. 8vo.   2 00

HOWE (H.) Historical Collections of Ohio. Containing a Collection of the most Interesting Facts, Traditions, Biographical Sketches, Anecdotes, etc., relating to its Local and General History. 8vo.   6 00

HUNT (W. E.) Historical Collections of Coshocton County, Ohio. 8vo.   3 00

HUSTON (R. G.) Journey in Honduras, and Jottings by the Way. Inter-Oceanic Railway. 8vo. Paper.   50

JACKSON (John D., M.D.) The Black Arts in Medicine, with an Anniversary Address. Edited by Dr. L. S. McMurtry. 12mo.   1 00

JASPER (T.) The Birds of North America. Colored Plates, drawn from Nature, with Descriptive and Scientific Letterpress. In 40 parts, $1.00 each; or, 2 vols. Royal 4to. Halfmorocco, $50 00; full morocco,   60 00
    The Same. Popular portion only with the Colored Plates.
    1 vol. Half morocco, $36.50; full morocco,   40 00

JORDAN (D. M.) Rosemary Leaves. A Collection of Poems. 18mo.   1 50

KELLER (M. J.) Elementary Perspective, explained and applied to Familiar Objects. Illustrated. 12mo.   1 00

KING (John). A Commentary on the Law and True Construction of the Federal Constitution. 8vo.   2 50

KLIPPART (J. H.) The Principles and Practice of Land Drainage. Illustrated. 12mo.   1 75

LAW (J.) Colonial History of Vincennes, Indiana, under the French, British, and American Governments. 12mo.   1 00

LLOYD (J. U.) The Chemistry of Medicines. Illus. 12mo. Cloth, $2 75; Sheep,   3 25

LLOYD (J. U.) Pharmaceutical Preparations; Elixirs, their History, Formulæ, and Methods of Preparation. 12mo. 1 25

LONGLEY (Elias). Eclectic Manual of Phonography. A Complete Guide to the Acquisition of Pitman's Phonetic Shorthand, with or without a Master. A new and carefully revised edition. 12mo. Stiff paper binding, 65c.; Cloth,   75

LONGLEY (Elias). The Reporter's Guide. Designed for Students in any Style of Phonography; in which are formulated for the first time in any work of the kind Rules for the Contraction of Words, Principles of Phrasing, and Methods of Abbreviation. Abundantly illustrated. 12mo.   2 00

LONGLEY (Elias). American Phonographic Dictionary, exhibiting the correct and actual Shorthand Forms for all the useful Words in the English Language, about 50,000 in number, and, in addition, many Foreign Terms; also, for 2,000 Geographical Names, and as many Family, Personal, and Noted Fictitious Names. 12mo.   2 50

LONGLEY (Elias). Every Reporter's Own Shorthand Dictionary The same as the above, but printed on writing paper, leaving out the Shorthand Forms and giving blank lines opposite each word, for the purpose of enabling writers of any System of Shorthand to put upon record, for convenient reference, the peculiar word-forms they employ. 12mo. 2 50

LONGLEY (Elias). Compend of Phonography, presenting a Table of all Alphabetical Combinations, Hooks, Circles, Loops, etc., at one view, also, Complete Lists of Word-signs and Contracted Word-forms, with Rules for Contracting Words for the Use of Writers of all Styles of Phonography. 12mo. Paper. 25

LONGLEY (Elias). The Phonetic Reader and Writer, containing Reading Exercises, with Translations on opposite pages, which form Writing Exercises. 12mo. 25

LONGLEY (Elias). Phonographic Chart. 28 x 42 inches. 50

McBRIDE (J.) Pioneer Biography; Sketches of the Lives of some of the Early Settlers of Butler County, Ohio. 2 vols. 8vo. $6 50. Large paper. Imp. 8vo. 13 00

McLAUGHLIN (M. Louise). China Painting. A Practical Manual for the Use of Amateurs in the Decoration of Hard Porcelain. Sq. 12mo. Boards. 75

McLAUGHLIN (M. Louise). Pottery Decoration: being a Practical Manual of Underglaize Painting. Sq. 12mo. Boards. 1 00

McLAUGHLIN (M. Louise). Suggestions for China Painters. Sq. 12mo. Boards. 1 00

MACLEAN (J. P.) The Mound Builders, and an Investigation into the Archæology of Butler County, Ohio. Illus. 12mo. 1 50

MACLEAN (J P.) A Manual of the Antiquity of Man. Illustrated. 12mo. 1 00

MACLEAN (J. P) Mastodon, Mammoth, and Man. Illustrated. 12mo. 60

MACLEAN (J P.) The Worship of the Reciprocal Principles of Nature among the Ancient Hebrews. 18mo. Paper. 25

MANSFIELD (E. D.) Personal Memories, Social, Political, and Literary 1803-43. 12mo. 2 00

MANYPENNY (G. W.) Our Indian Wards. A History and Discussion of the Indian Question. 8vo. 3 00

MAY (Col. J.) Journal and Letters of, relative to Two Journeys to the Ohio Country, 1788 and 1779. 8vo. 2 00

METTENHEIMER (H. J.) Safety Book-keeping. Being a Complete Exposition of Book-keeper's Frauds—how Committed, how discovered, how prevented; with other Suggestions of Value to Merchants and Book-keepers in the Management of Accounts. 18mo. Cloth. 1 00

MINOR (T. C., M.D.) Child-bed Fever. Erysipelas and Puerperal Fever, with a Short Account of both Diseases. 8vo. 2 00

MINOR (T. C., M.D.) Scarlatina Statistics of the United States. 8vo. Paper. 50

MORGAN (Appleton). The Shakespearean Myth; or, William Shakespeare and Circumstantial Evidence. 12mo. 2 00

MORGAN (Appleton). Some Shakespearean Commentators. 12mo. Paper. 75

NAME AND ADDRESS BOOK. A Blank Book, with Printed Headings and Alphabetical Marginal Index, for Recording the Names and Addresses of Professional, Commercial, and Family Correspondents. 8vo. 1 00

NASH (Simeon). Crime and the Family. 12mo.   1 25
NERINCKX (Rev. Charles). Life of, with Early Catholic Missions
    in Kentucky; the Society of Jesus; the Sisterhood of Loretto,
    etc. By Rev. G. P. Maes. 8vo.   2 50
NICHOLS (G. W.) The Cincinnati Organ; with a Brief Descrip-
    tion of the Cincinnati Music Hall. 12mo. Paper.   25
OHIO VALLEY HISTORICAL MISCELLANIES. I. Memorandums of a
    Tour made by Josiah Espy, in the States of Ohio, and Ken-
    tucky, and Indian Territory, in 1805. II. Two Western Cam-
    paigns in the War of 1812–13: 1. Expedition of Capt. H. Brush,
    with Supplies for General Hull. 2. Expedition of Gov. Meigs,
    for the relief of Fort Meigs. By Samuel Williams. III. The
    Leatherwood God: an account of the Appearance and Preten-
    tions of J. C. Dylks in Eastern Ohio, in 1828. By R. H.
    Taneyhill. 1 vol. 8vo. $2 50. Large paper,   5 00
ONCE A YEAR; or, The Doctor's Puzzle. By E. B. S. 16mo. 1 00
OSBORN (H. S.) Ancient Egypt in the Light of Modern Discov-
    eries. Illustrated. 12mo.   1 25
PHISTERER (Captain Frederick). The National Guardsman: on
    Guard and Kindred Duties. 24mo. Leather.   75
PHYSICIAN'S POCKET CASE RECORD PRESCRIPTION BOOK.   35
PHYSICIAN'S GENERAL LEDGER. Half Russia.   4 00
PIATT (John J.) Penciled Fly-Leaves. A Book of Essays in
    Town and Country. Sq. 16mo.   1 00
POOLE (W. F.) Anti-Slavery Opinions before 1800. An Essay.
    8vo. Paper, 75c.; Cloth,   1 25
PRENTICE (Geo. D.) Poems of, collected and edited, with Bio-
    graphical Sketch, by John J. Piatt. 12mo.   2 00
QUICK (R. H.) Essays on Educational Reformers. Schools of
    the Jesuits: Ascham, Montaigne, Ratich, Milton; Comenius;
    Locke; Rousseau's Emile; Basidow and the Philanthropin,
    etc. 12mo.   1 50
RANCK (G. W.) History of Lexington, Kentucky. Its Early
    Annals and Recent Progress, etc. 8vo.   4 00
REEMELIN (C.) The Wine-Maker's Manual. A Plain, Practical
    Guide to all the Operations for the Manufacture of Still and
    Sparkling Wines. 12mo.   1 25
REEMELIN (C.) A Treatise on Politics as a Science. 8vo.   1 50
REEMELIN (C.) A Critical Review of American Politics. 8vo. 3 50
REEMELIN (C.) Historical Sketch of Green Township, Hamilton
    County, Ohio. 8vo. Paper.   1 25
RIVES (E. M. D.) A Chart of the Physiological Arrangement
    of Cranial Nerves. Printed in large type, on a sheet 28 x 15
    inches. Folded, in cloth case.   50
ROBERT (Karl). Charcoal Drawing without a Master. A Com-
    plete Treatise in Landscape Drawing in Charcoal, with Lessons
    and Studies after Allonge. Translated by E. H. Appleton.
    Illustrated. 8vo.   1 00
ROY (George). Generalship; or, How I Managed my Husband.
    A tale. 18mo. Paper, 50c.; Cloth.   1 00
ROY (George). The Art of Pleasing. A Lecture. 12mo. Pa-
    per.   25

Roy (George). The Old, Old Story. A Lecture. **12mo.** Paper. 25

Russell (A. P.) Thomas Corwin. A Sketch. 16mo. 1 00

Russell (Wm.) Scientific Horseshoeing for the Different Diseases of the Feet. Illustrated. 8vo. 1 00

Sattler (Eric E.) The History of Tuberculosis from the time of Sylvius to the Present Day. Translated, in part, with additions, from the German of Dr. Arnold Spina, First Assistant in the Laboratory of Professor Stricker, of Vienna: including also Dr. Robert Koch's Experiments, and the more recent Investigations of Dr. Spina on the Subject. 12mo. 1 25

Sayler (J. A.) American Form Book. A Collection of Legal and Business Forms, embracing Deeds, Mortgages, Leases, Bonds, Wills, Contracts, Bills of Exchange, Promissory Notes, Checks, Bills of Sale, Receipts, and other Legal Instruments, prepared in accordance with the Laws of the several States; with Instructions for drawing and executing the same. For Professional and Business Men. 8vo. 2 00

Sheets (Mary R.) My Three Angels: Faith, Hope, and Love. With full-page illustration. By E. D. Grafton. 4to. Cloth. Gilt. 5 00

Skinner (J. R.) The Source of Measures. A Key to the Hebrew-Egyptian Mystery in the Source of Measures, etc. 8vo. 5 00

Smith (Col. James). A Reprint of an Account of the Remarkable Occurrences in his Life and Travels, during his Captivity with the Indians in the years 1755, '56, '57, '58, and '59, etc. 8vo. $2 50. Large paper. 5 00

Stanton (H.) Jacob Brown and other Poems. 12mo. 1 50

St. Clair Papers. A Collection of the Correspondence and other papers of General Arthur St. Clair, Governor of the Northwest Territory. Edited, with a Sketch of his Life and Public Services, by William Henry Smith. 2 vols. 8vo. 6 00

Strauch (A.) Spring Grove Cemetery, Cincinnati: its History and Improvements, with Observations on Ancient and Modern Places of Sepulture. The text beautifully printed with ornamental colored borders, and photographic illustrations. 4to. Cloth. Gilt. 15 00

An 8vo. edition, without border and illustrations. 2 00

Studer (J. H.) Columbus, Ohio: its History, Resources, and Progress, from its Settlement to the Present Time. 12mo. 2 00

Taneyhill (R. H.) The Leatherwood God: an account of the Appearance and Pretensions of Joseph C. Dylks in Eastern Ohio, in 1826. 12mo. Paper. 30

Ten Brook (A.) American State Universities. Their Origin and Progress. A History of the Congressional University Land Grants. A particular account of the Rise and Development of the University of Michigan, and Hints toward the future of the American University System. 8vo. 2 00

Tilden (Louise W.) Karl and Gretchen's Christmas. Illustrated. Square 12mo. 75

Tilden (Louise W.) Poem, Hymn, and Mission Band Exercises. Written and arranged for the use of Foreign Missionary Societies and Mission Bands. Square 12mo. Paper. 25

TRENT (Capt. Wm.) Journal of, from Logstown to Pickawillany, in 1752. Edited by A. T. Goodman. 8vo. 2 50

TRIPLER (C. S., M. D.) and BLACKMAN (G. C., M. D.) Handbook for the Military Surgeon. 12mo. 1 00

TYLER DAVIDSON FOUNTAIN. History and Description of the Tyler Davidson Fountain, Donated to the City of Cincinnati, by Henry Probasco. 18mo. Paper. 25

VAGO (A. L.) Instructions in the Art of Modeling in Clay. With an Appendix on Modeling in Foliage, etc., for Pottery and Architectural Decorations, by Benn Pitman, of Cincinnati School of Design. Illustrated. Square 12mo. 1 00

VAN HORNE (T. B.) The History of the Army of the Cumberland; its Organization, Campaigns, and Battles. *Library Edition.* 2 vols. With Atlas of 22 maps, compiled by Edward Ruger. 8vo. Cloth, $8 00; Sheep, $10 00; Half Morocco, $12 00. *Popular Edition.* Containing the same Text as the Library Edition, but only one map. 2 vols. 8vo. Cloth. 5 00

VENABLE (W. H.) June on the Miami, and other Poems. Second edition, 18mo. 1 50

VOORHEES (D. W.) Speeches of, embracing his most prominent Forensic, Political, Occasional, and Literary Addresses. Compiled by his son, C. S. Voorhees, with a Biographical Sketch and Portrait. 8vo. 5 00

WALKER (C. M.) History of Athens County, Ohio, and incidentally of the Ohio Land Company, and the First Settlement of the State at Marietta, etc. 8vo. $6 00. Large Paper. 2 vols. $12 00. Popular Edition. 4 00

WALTON (G. E.) Hygiene and Education of Infants; or, How to take care of Babies. 24mo. Paper. 25

WARD (Durbin). American Coinage and Currency. An Essay read before the Social Science Congress, at Cincinnati, May 22, 1878. 8vo. Paper. 10

WEBB (F.) and JOHNSTON (M. C.) An Improved Tally-Book for the use of Lumber Dealers. 18mo. 50

WHITTAKER (J. T., M. D.) Physiology; Preliminary Lectures. Illustrated. 12mo 1 75

WILLIAMS (A. D., M. D.) Diseases of the Ear, including Necessary Anatomy of the Organ. 8vo. 3 50

YOUNG (A.) History of Wayne County, Indiana, from its First Settlement to the Present Time. 8vo. 2 00

LAW TREATISES AND REPORTS.

ADKINSON (F.) Township and Town Officer's Guide for the State of Indiana. 12mo. Net. Cloth, $2 00; Sheep. 2 50

BARTON (C.) History of a Suit in Equity. Revised and enlarged. 8vo. 2 50

BATES (C.) Ohio Pleadings, Parties, and Forms under the Code. 2 vols. 8vo. Net. 12 00

BIBLE IN THE PUBLIC SCHOOLS. Arguments in favor and against, with Decision of the Cincinnati Superior Court. 8vo. Cloth. 2 00

BIBLE IN THE PUBLIC SCHOOLS. The arguments in favor of, and
  against. Separate. Paper. Each, 50
BLOOM (S. S.) Popular Edition of the Laws of Ohio, in Force
  June, 1882. Net. Cloth, $3 00; Sheep, 4 00
BOND (L. H.) Reports of Cases Decided in the Circuit and
  District Courts of the United States for the Southern District
  of Ohio. 2 vols. 8vo. 14 00
BURNS (H.) An Index or Abbreviated Digest of the Supreme
  Court Reports of the State of Indiana, from 1st Blackford to
  77th Indiana, inclusive. 8vo. Net. 5 00
CARLTON (A. B.) The Law of Homicide; together with the Cel-
  ebrated Trial of Judge E. C. Wilkinson, Dr. B. R. Wilkinson,
  and J. Murdaugh, for the Murder of John Rothwell and A. H.
  Meeks, including the Indictments, the Evidence, and Speeches
  of Hon. S. S. Prentiss, Hon. Ben. Hardin, E. J. Bullock, Judge
  John Rowan, Col. Geo. Robertson, and John B. Thompson, of
  Counsel, in full. 8vo. Net. 2 50
CINCINNATI SUPERIOR COURT REPORTER. 2 vols. 8vo. Net. 10 00
  See also Handy, Disney.
CONSTITUTION OF THE UNITED STATES, with the Fifteen Amend-
  ments, Declaration of Independence, etc. 8vo. Paper. 25
COX (R.) American Trade Mark Cases. A Compilation of all
  reported Trade Mark cases decided in the United States Courts
  prior to 1871. 8vo. 8 00
CURWEN (M. E.) Manual of Abstracts of Title to Real Property.
  Edited by W. H. Whittaker. 12mo. 2 00
DAVIS (E. A.) New Digest of the Decisions of the Supreme
  Court of Indiana, to 1875. 2 vols. 8vo. Net. 12 00
DISNEY'S REPORTS. Cincinnati Superior Court. 2 vols. 8vo.
  Net. 10 00
FISHER (S. S.) Reports of Patent Cases decided in the Circuit
  Courts of the United States, 1843–1873. 6 vols. 8vo. Vols.
  3 to 6, each. Net. 25 00
FISHER (W. H.) Reports of Patent Cases decided in the Courts
  of the United States, 1827–1851. 10 00
FISHER (R. A.) Digest of English Patent, Trade Mark, and
  Copyright Cases. Edited by Henry Hooper. 8vo. 4 00
FORTESCUE (Sir John). De Laudibus Legum Angliæ. A Treatise
  in Commendation of the Laws of England. 8vo. Cloth. 3 00
GIAUQUE (F.) The Election Laws of the United States. Being
  a Compilation of all the Constitutional Provisions and Laws
  of the United States relating to Elections, the Elective Fran-
  chise, to Citizenship, and to the Naturalization of Aliens.
  With Notes of Decisions affecting the same. 8vo. Paper.
  75c.; Cloth. 1 00
GIAUQUE (F.) Ohio Election Laws. 8vo. Paper, $1.00; Cloth, 1 50
GIAUQUE (F.) Manual for Road Supervisors in Ohio. 16mo.
  Boards. 25
GIAUQUE (F.) Manual for Assignees and Insolvent Debtors in
  Ohio. Net. Cloth, $2 00; Sheep, 2 50
GIAUQUE (F.) Manual for Guardians in Ohio. Net. Cloth,
  $2 00; Sheep, 2 50

GIAUQUE (F.) A complete Manual of the Road Laws of Ohio in force 1883, with Forms and Notes of Decisions. *In press.*

GIAUQUE (F.) and McCLURE (H. B.) Dower and Curtesy Tables, for ascertaining, on the basis of the Carlisle Tables of Mortality, the present value of vested and contingent rights of Dower and Curtesy, and of other Life Estates. 8vo. Net. 5 00

HANDY'S REPORTS. Cincinnati Superior Court. 2 vols. in 1. 8vo. Net. 5 00

HANOVER (M. D.) A Practical Treatise on the Law relating to Horses. Second edition. 8vo. 4 00

HARRIS (S. F.) Principles of the Criminal Law. Edited by Hon. M. F. Force. 8vo. Net. 4 00

INDIANA LAWS. Being Acts and Joint Resolutions of the General Assembly of the State of Indiana, passed at the Regular Session, which was begun and held at Indianapolis, on Thursday, the fourth day of January, 1883, and adjourned without day on Monday, the fifth day of March, 1883. Edited, printed, published, and circulated under authority of law, and with the Secretary of State's authentication. S. R. Downey, Editor. 8vo. 1 00

KENTUCKY REPORTS. Reports of cases decided in the Court of Appeals of Kentucky. 1785–1878. 76 vols. in 61.

KING (J.) A Commentary on the Law and True Construction of the Federal Constition. 8vo. 2 50

McDONALD (D.) Treatise on the Law relating to the Powers and Duties of Justices and Constables in Indiana. Edited by L. O. Schroeder. 8vo. Net. 6 00

MATTHEWS (Stanley). A Summary of the Law of Partnership. For use of Business Men. 12mo. Cloth, $1 25; Sheep, 1 50

McLEAN (J.) Reports of Cases decided in the Circuit Court of the United States for the Seventh District. 1829–1555. 6 vols. 8vo. Vols. 2, 4, 5, 6. Each, 6 50

MONTESQUIEU (Baron De). The Spirit of Laws. Translated from the French by Thomas Nugent. New edition, with Memoir. 2 vols. 8vo. Cloth. 6 00

MORGAN (J. A.) An English Version of Legal Maxims, with the Original Forms. Alphabetically arranged, and an Index of Subjects. Second edition. 12mo. Cloth. Net. 2 00

NASH (S.) Pleading and Practice under the Codes of Ohio, New York, Kansas, and Nebraska. Fourth edition, 2 vols. 8vo. Net. 10 00

OHIO AND OHIO STATE REPORTS. Reports of Cases decided in the Supreme Court of Ohio. 1821–1880. 55 vols. Net 137 50

OHIO STATUTES. Embracing:
Curwen's Statutes at Large, 1833–1860. 4 vols. 8vo. Net. 20 00
Swan & Critchfield's Revised Statutes, 1860. 2 vols. 8vo. Net. 5 00
Sayler's Statutes at Large, 1860–1875. 4 vols. 8vo. 20 00

PECK (H. D.) The Law of Municipal Corporations in the State of Ohio. Second edition. 8vo. 5 00

PECK (H. D.) The Township-Officer's Guide of Ohio. Second edition Net. Cloth, $2 00; Sheep, 2 50

Pollock (F.) Principles of Contract at Law and in Equity. Edited by G. H. Wald. 8vo. Net. 6 00

Raff (G. W.) Guide to Executors and Administrators in the State of Ohio. Sixth edition. Edited and enlarged by F. Giauque. 12mo. Cloth, $2 00; Sheep, 2 50

Raff (G. W.) Manual of Pensions, Bounty, and Pay. 1789–1863. 12mo. **2 00**

Raff (G. W.) War Claimant's Guide. Laws relating to Pensions, Bounty, etc. War of 1861–1865. 8vo. **4 00**

Reinhard (G. L.) The Criminal Law of the State of Indiana, with Precedents, Forms for Writs, Docket Entries, etc. 8vo. 2 50

Saint Germain (C.) The Doctor and Student; or, Dialogues between a Doctor of Divinity and a Student in the Laws of England, containing the grounds of those Laws. Revised and corrected. 8vo. Cloth. 3 00

Saunders (T. W.) A Treatise upon the Law of Negligence. With notes of American Cases. 8vo. **2 50**

Sayler (J. R.) American Form Book; a Collection of Legal and Business Forms for Professional and Business Men. 8vo. Cloth. Net. 2 0)

Stanton (R. H.) A New Digest of the Kentucky Decisions; embracing all Cases decided by the Appellate Courts, from 1785 to 1877. Second edition. 2 vols. 8vo. Net. 6 00

Stanton (R. H.) A Practical Treatise on the Law relating to Justices of the Peace, etc., in Kentucky. Third edition. 8vo. 7 50

Stanton (R. H.) Manual for the Use of Executors, Administrators, Guardians, etc., in Kentucky. Second edition. 12mo. 1 75

Swan (J. R.) Pleadings and Precedents, under the Code of Ohio. 8vo. 6 00

Swan (J. R.) Treatise on the Law relating to the Powers and Duties of Justices of the Peace, etc., in the State of Ohio. Eleventh edition. 8vo. Net. **6 00**

Swan (J. R.) and Plumb (P. B.) Treatise on the Law relating to the Powers and Duties of Justices, etc., in Kansas. 8vo. 5 00

Walker (J. B.) and Bates (C.) A new Digest of Ohio Decisions. Second edition. 2 vols. 8vo. Net. 12 00
Vol. 3, 1874–1882. By C. Bates. Net. 5 00

Warren (M.) Criminal Law and Forms. Third edition. 8vo. 5 00

Wells (J. C.) Treatise on the Separate Property of Married Women, under the recent Enabling Acts. Second edition. 8vo. 6 00

Wells (J. C.) A Manual of the Laws relating to County Commissioners in the State of Ohio, with carefully prepared Forms, and References to the Decisions of the Supreme Court. Net. **3 50**

Wild (E. N.) Journal Entries under the Codes of Civil and Criminal Procedure. With Notes of Decisions. Second edition. 8vo. 4 00

WILCOX (J. A.)   The General Railroad Laws of the State of Ohio, in force January, 1874.   8vo.   5 00
WILSON (M. F.)   The New Criminal Code of Ohio, with Forms and Precedents, Digest of Decisions, etc.   Second edition. 8vo.   Net. 5 00
WORKS (John D.)   Indiana Practice, Pleadings, and Forms. 2 vols. 8vo.   Net. 12 00

NASH (Simeon).   Lawyer's Case Docket, containing printed Headings, and blank spaces for names of Parties, Memoranda of all the Proceedings, with full printed Instructions, and an Index.   Crown size.   Half roan, $3.75; Full Sheep.   4 50
LAWYER'S COLLECTION DOCKET.   With convenient Ruling, printed Headings, Index, etc.   4to.   Half Russia.   3 50
ATTORNEY'S POCKET DOCKET.   Ruled and Printed for number of Case, Parties, and kind of Action, Witnesses, etc., with room for 150 cases.   Pocket size.   Morocco.   1 00
CHANGEABLE POCKET DOCKET.   The Docket paper is furnished separately, and so arranged that it may be subsequently bound in one volume.   Paper, 50c. per quire.   Morocco case, with pocket and band.   2 00
NOTARY'S OFFICIAL REGISTER.   Being a Record of Protests and other Official Transactions.   4to.   2 quires.   Half sheep, $2 00; 3 quires, half russia.   3 00
COLLECTION RECEIPT BOOK.   The Book of Collection Receipts, which is bound in the form of a check book, contains the stub in which is preserved a record of the transaction, and a printed receipt, giving parties, date, interest, indorsers, credits, etc., which is torn off and sent to your correspondent. Book of 50 receipts, 40c.; 100 receipts, 75c.; 200 (two to a page).   1 25
A Catalogue of Legal Blanks will be sent on application.

LAWYER'S OFFICE DOCKET.

The Lawyer's Office Docket.   Embracing the History of each Case, and the Proceedings thereon, together with a Digest of the Principles of Law involved, and References to Authorities. With Index and Memoranda.   Quarto.   212 pages.   Half russia. Cloth sides.   Net.   3 50

THE UNITED STATES COMMISSIONER'S DOCKET.

Docket for Commissioners of the United States Circuit Courts, embracing a Full Record of the Proceeding in each Case, with Schedule of Costs, and an Index of Cases.   Quarto.   Half russia. Net.   3 75

www.ingramcontent.com/pod-product-compliance
Lightning Source LLC
Chambersburg PA
CBHW030024030726
47499CB00008B/3107